Damn Right It Hurts!

Damn Right It Hurts!

✦

A Virginia Hillbilly Becomes a World War II Hero

Wade Gilley

iUniverse, Inc.

New York Lincoln Shanghai

Damn Right It Hurts!
A Virginia Hillbilly Becomes a World War II Hero

iUniverse, Inc.

For information address:
iUniverse, Inc.
2021 Pine Lake Road, Suite 100
Lincoln, NE 68512
www.iuniverse.com

ISBN: 0-595-32094-5

Printed in the United States of America

Contents

Acknowledgements

Damn Right It Hurts is the story of Russell "Russ" Gilley's life from his early years to his Army enlistment during World War II to December 1947, when his body was sent home to its final resting place in Fries, Virginia. Russ Gilley was Wade Gilley's uncle. According to fellow GI Ron Kraemer, "Damn Right It Hurts" were Russ Gilley's last words. Yet those words also speak of the torment and anguish of Oda Gilley, the author's grandmother, who grieved for the remainder of her life over the loss of her baby son.

This book reflects Wade Gilley's memories as a 6-year-old witness to a dramatic event that forever changed the lives of those closest to him. The background and many of the stories are true. The dialogue generally connotes what the author heard and remembers as a child.

Damn Right It Hurts was a collaborative effort. The timely intervention in 1999 of J. L. Seel of Belgium encouraged Wade Gilley to fulfill the promise he had made to his family to research and write the story of Russ Gilley. The recollections of two of the author's aunts, help from his cousins Helen "Toodie" Davenport Blevins and Rex Gilley and his sister Mickey Gilley Weikle, and insights from Russ Gilley's high school friends, Ilas Gallimore and Alan "Birddog" Jennings were invaluable. Special thanks also go to scientist turned novelist, Dr. Jessica Andersen, for her support and guidance.

Last, but never least, the author thanks his constant and constructive critic of 43 years, Nanna Beverly Gilley, without whose support this book would have been impossible.

BRONZE STAR MEDAL

◆

Private First Class Russell J. Gilley

"For heroic action in connection with military operations
against the enemy on
16, December 1944, in Germany"

◆   ◆   ◆

When overwhelming superior forces surrounded his unit, Private First
Class Gilley and a comrade volunteered to attempt the seemingly
impossible task of piercing the enemy's ring of steel to contact friendly
units. By utilizing every bit of cover and concealment, both men made
the trip safely. After reporting his valuable information on the disposition of hostile forces, Private First Class Gilley resumed the fight
against the enemy.
By his heroic action, Private First Class Gilley reflects credit upon himself and the armed forces."

◆   ◆   ◆

U. S. Army, 1945

Elsenborn Ridge, December 1944

"You're damn right it hurts," answered the bloody, mud covered young GI. "Whiz, God damn it hurts."

The young baby faced GI known as "Whiz Kid" ran to meet the sled being carried back behind the firing lines to a forward aid station. He recognized his friend, Private First Class Russell Gilley, known to some as "Cookie." Russ was lying on his back, his chest and side bloody, his lower body shielded from view by an army medic. The medic administered a shot of morphine to deaden the pain and to prevent the shock that killed so many wounded American boys in World War II.

"Cookie? Russ? That you? What happened, Russ boy?" Whiz Kid Carson grabbed hold of the sled and shouted rapid-fire support over the deafening noise of the bombardment from the German mortars and 88s. "Hang in there! Hang in there, boy."

When there was a brief lull in the noise, he leaned close to his friend.

"Does it hurt?" he asked.

"You're damn right it hurts," answered the bloody, mud covered young GI, his eyes filled with pain. "Whiz, God damn it hurts."

A Drink of Warm Cow's Milk

"Ode, Ode, what's going on? What happened to Russell? Is he hurt?" The large man in bibbed overalls jumped the barbed wire fence and strode through the vegetable garden, straight to where his wife and their baby son sat on the ground outside the old barn...."

◆　　◆　　◆

Russ felt the nurse shaking him out of his stupor. "Farm boy, do you want a drink of warm milk?"

The question woke him up—kind of. He turned to look at the nurse in her dirty, bloody, army-green pullover. *Warm milk? Is Mom here with a cup of just-milked cow's milk for me? Is Mom here?* He sipped from the cup and let the nurse ease him back into the bed, then fell back into his fitful sleep. Painful too, whenever the morphine shot was light. God, it hurt awful.

Though a part of him knew he was lying in a tent on the frontlines of the war against Germany, just east of Elsenborn Ridge, another part of him was a fly on the wall looking down on a scene from fifteen years earlier in 1929. He was just five years old, and that was the day his momma, Oda Gilley, had gotten in trouble milking the cow.

It was Sunday and they were getting ready to go to church. Mom organized the family: four girls and the three boys, including fifteen-year-old Wood and five-year-old Russ.

Before church, which was an all-day affair, Oda Gilley had lots of organizing to do. The girls had to make sure everything was set for Monday, because they'd be back late at night. The hard-shell Baptist Sundays started mid-morning and the preaching and singing lasted

2

well into the evening. The two bigger girls, Bell and Pearl, had everybody moving around, except for Bill, who'd already had a little run-in
with Mom and was hiding out until it was time to leave. Daddy and
their elder brother, Wood, were working on the Model T truck that
would haul the entire family from Washington County, Virginia up
the Blue Ridge Mountains to Konnarock, which was almost into the
North Carolina mountains where Oda had grown up. It was a long
ride and everyone knew Bill and the older girls would rather be somewhere else, but it would be a real family get-together.

The important thing to Russ, as he remembered the day from his
bed in a faraway land, had been how his mom had scrubbed him from
top to bottom before putting on his best hand-me-down clothes. They
might have been Bill's, or maybe even one of the girls', but that didn't
much matter to a five-year-old.

"There," his momma crooned, "boy, you look good! Uncle Ed and
everybody else there are going to be proud of my baby boy. Big boy,
Big Russell."

Then she turned, grabbed a milk bucket off the porch and headed
for the barn. "Come on, Russ, come on and we'll get some of that
warm cow's milk you love so much. Come on." She was walking so
fast; Russ had to trot to even hope to keep up.

As soon as she got to the barn, Oda tied the cow to a post, placed
some chop into an old rusted bucket and plopped the meal down in
front of the grateful creature.

As the cow munched away, Oda squatted down and began milking,
starting with the over-full back tits. The two-gallon bucket was more
than half full before she slowed to an easier stroke and glanced over at
her baby boy.

"Russ! See that tin cup I left on the windowsill over there? Pick it up
and hand it to me. Hand it here and I'll milk you some warm and
goody milk. That is just what you need."

Oda's lanky shape was evident as she squatted and continued to
milk; her knees were folded almost over her head like a grasshopper. At

that point in her life, Oda Gilley was thirty-eight years old, a tall, thin, dark woman of Cherokee descent. She had learned at a young age to take charge of things in her life. That would always be the case with her baby boy, too, but there she wouldn't always prevail. Russ, as more than one person believed, was Oda's Waterloo.

Little Russell dashed over to the barn window, picked up the tin cup and hurried back to hand it to his momma. He watched as she squirted the streams of warm, white milk into it. That was his milk, he knew. They'd done this before.

"Uh, uh, Mom? Milk?" he pleaded, urging his mom to hurry. He could hardly wait.

Oda handed the cup to him and returned to her milking. He leaned against her as he drank. It was just the two of them. It was special.

Just about then, a greenhead fly landed on the old orange and white spotted Guernsey's belly and took a bite. The cow moved her right hind-leg to scratch the big fly off her stomach, her hoof clipping the bucket of milk.

Oda turned loose of the tit and whacked the cow on the side. "Stop that! You behave," she said, and gave the old cow another whack.

Something was causing that cow's belly to itch that evening. She jerked her right hoof back and clawed hard at her belly button, this time hitting the bucket a good lick on the way up. Milk splashed. Oda jumped back and stumbled, and the cow kicked hard at her belly again.

This time, her backswing struck Russ in the chest. His breath *whooshed* out as the hoof caught the front of his new, clean Sunday bibs and jerked him headfirst into the milk bucket!

Oda squealed and yanked him out of harm's way, in the process shoving him back, back, back…right into a pile of fresh cow shit.

Russ ended up just where that old fly had probably wanted to be to start with.

Big Webb Gilley came running up, wondering what had happened. Oda was sitting flat on the ground with her knees up around her head, clutching her five-year-old. The cow was chewing her cud.

"Ode? Ode? What in the world happened?" (Ode was Webb Gilley's nickname for his wife Oda.) He checked the two of them out, but couldn't find anything wrong with them except more than a little dirt. "I told you I'd do the milking as soon as we got the oil changed in the truck," he said. "Why couldn't you wait?"

Well, Oda just didn't like to wait on someone else to do what she needed done. That was why she couldn't wait. That wasn't Oda Osborne Gilley's way. Webb must've known that without asking, but he asked anyway. What else could he say? It was probably that or burst out laughing, which would never have done.

"How's Russ?" Webb asked, and turned to Russ. "You okay, son?"

"Shit, shut up Webb," Oda barked at her husband. "I checked him, the boy's okay. Where are we going to get the milk to feed him? That's what I want to know."

"Oh, we'll stop on the way to the church at Konnarock. That guy beside the Jot'em Down at the crossroads, he'll have some. We'll get some. Just you get up and wash off. You look awful."

Oda stood and looked at the boy she would always consider her baby. "Come on Russ, let's us start over," she whispered. "We'll get you that warm milk later."

◆   ◆   ◆

The medic looked at the feverish young GI on the table. "What happened?" he asked the nurse. "Is he out of his head again? Did you give him his penicillin and the morphine?"

"Yes, he's had his meds for the night. I just asked him if he wanted a drink of the warm milk that mud-face Ralph Hill got from a captured Belgian cow. He looked as though he knew exactly what I was offering and took one long sip before easing back down on the bed. That milk seemed to really put him at peace." She gazed down for a long moment and smiled. "He hasn't been thrashing around so much tonight. He seems to be in another world with some people named Wood and Oda and Reba and Ruby."

The medic's grimace betrayed his exhaustion. "We should all be so lucky—to be in another world."

◆   ◆   ◆

In his memories, Russell Gilley was safe and warm with his mom in the front seat of the truck with his daddy and Reba. He could look over his mom's shoulder through the window, the one without glass, and see Wood and Bill and his sisters back in the truck bed.

They were on their way to Konnarock to church. They would get some warm milk at the Jot'em down. Daddy had promised. It was so peaceful and secure as little Russell sat there with his momma and daddy.

"He's groaning again. What are you doing?" the doctor asked the nurse.

"Just rubbing his lips with a little of this ointment. They're dry and cracking."

"So what is he saying?"

"Don't know for sure, it seems like he's back with his momma Oda again." She paused, and then whispered, "Wish more of these poor boys would dream of their mommas. It seems to help."

◆   ◆   ◆

"Where's my butter crock?" Oda asked her three tow-headed children as Baby Russ, Ruby and Reba collected around, watching with watering mouths and wondering whether they'd get a taste of butter.

Oda had just finished churning cream to make real cow's butter, one of the delicacies of country farm life in the western mountains of Virginia during the Great Depression.

For several days, she had saved the cream that rose overnight when new cow's milk was left in a Ball jar in the cool trough water. Each morning, she ladled the cream off and stored it in a warm place where it soured. Then she churned it to separate the butter and buttermilk, dipped the congealed butter out with her hands, dropped it in a clean pan, and used a wooden spoon to collect the last bits of butter. She had to get it all. Finally, she used her careful, skilled hands to knead the big mound of yellowish-white butter in a pan of cold water to further separate the remaining buttermilk. Several times, she poured off the milk-colored water and refilled the pan with fresh cold spring water until there was nothing left except cold water and pure milk fat.

Then she packed the butter into wooden molds, squeezing it to remove that last bit of milk and any air bubbles. One by one, she emptied the molds onto a shiny, well-worn (and clean) wooden board until all the butter was turned into glistening shapes, sitting in a row. The old handcrafted wooden molds with their moveable tops each had a distinct design that ended up pressed into each individual pound of fresh, wonderful cow's butter. This butter would last the family for days.

The fascinated children watched Oda through the entire process. The girls in particular wanted to get their hands on that dasher and then on the butter itself. This couldn't have pleased Oda more, as they soon would take the chore off her list.

On the day Russ remembered, his mother had just reached the point of being ready to transfer the butter into her huge stone crock. That crock was one of the few things Oda had left from her own mother, who had died in childbirth when Oda was just three years old. The crock was a rare family heirloom in those hardscrabble parts and times.

Best of all (at least to the children), it would contain the butter. They could picture it on their breakfast biscuits and supper corn bread. They could even see themselves dipping their fingers in to a room-softened mold left on the kitchen table as they went in and out of the house. (Of course, they could only manage this when Oda was distracted, but they dreamed anyway.)

Once the butter was in the crock, Rube would take it to the springhouse, where it would be kept fresh in running spring water. Meanwhile Oda would complete her task by placing the semi-sour buttermilk into Ball jars, which would also be carried to the springhouse. The adults would enjoy this more than the children. But first she needed that crock.

"Rube? Where's my crock?"

"Momma, I don't know where it is!"

"Rebe?"

"Mom, what butter crock are you talking about?"

"Reba Gilley, you know where it is, and don't tell me that you don't."

This exclamation was followed by silence. Ruby, Reba, and Russ stared at the beautiful mounds of rich yellow butter, trying to ignore Oda, who had been working for more than an hour and was anxious to finish.

Always one to do it herself, Oda stalked into the kitchen to find the crock. It was nowhere to be seen. She moved down to the springhouse. It wasn't there either.

Upon returning, she saw her children toeing the dirt. They knew, and she knew they knew.

"Rube, I want that crock, now! Have you all done something with it? Oh *my God,* have you broken it?

"Momma, I have it," six-year-old Russ stepped up to report.

"Russell, you have it? I don't think so."

"Yes, I do. It's…it's up in the bedroom."

"What in the Sam Hill is it doing up there? That's what I want to know! Go get it. Right now, boy! And don't you drop it and break it or I'll skin you alive," she shouted. There was a hint of a smile on her face, though, as she watched her chubby son running to get the crock.

Moments later, Russ waddled up with the large crock cradled in his arms and placed it on the bench beside his momma. "Russ what have you done? Is something wrong with the crock?" He was so cautious with the precious crock that she had to ask.

Unable to resist speaking, Reba, in her life's role as Russell's protector, confessed. "Mom, Russ found a frog that he kept for a pet."

"What? A frog? What's that got to do with my butter crock?"

"Well, you see," Reba, continued, "he wanted to keep the frog under his bed and needed something to put it in."

Then it came to Oda. Restraining a smile she reached over and carefully lifted the lid off the crock. They all looked down and there it was…a green and brown toad.

"We named it the Toad's Abode," Reba declared, gesturing at the crock.

Oda could no longer restrain her smile. She spread her arms wide and gathered her three little ones in for a huge hug.

"You girls get that crock washed, and good. Then put the butter in the crock and take it to the springhouse Russ and I will get a quart jar and make some holes in its lid for that toad's new abode," she said, still smiling.

"We will, we will, Momma!" The girls dashed off to get the job done, happy now that the crisis was over and the butter was headed to the springhouse in its proper abode.

As Oda headed to the smoke house, Russell turned and ran after his sisters, forgetting the frog.

Momma would take care of it.

Going to School with Reba

"Do we know about his family?" The medic was asking the nurse about Russell, as they cared for a room full of wounded GIs, and it didn't take them long to identify with each one.

"Well, he keeps up a delirious conversation with his mom and someone named Rebe or Reba," the nurse said. "He talks about other people sometimes, but it's mainly the two of them."

"Well, all these guys have a mom, and some talk to them when they're delirious. Who is Rebe? Is she his girlfriend?"

"I don't think so. It seems like she's a buddy or a person he depends on for everything. It's almost like she's a second mother."

"Maybe Reba is his mother's name?"

"I don't think so," the nurse said, shaking her head. "Sometimes he talks to both of them at the same time."

Under heavy medication, mainly morphine for the pain, Russ heard their conversation.

"Rebe took me to school," he said.

"Did you hear that!" the nurse exclaimed. "He's telling us who Rebe is. Russell, Russell, she took you to school? What do you mean?"

Russ had drifted off again, thinking about going to school that first day with his big sister Reba holding his hand.

◆   ◆   ◆

"Mom, why didn't you let me go to school last year?" Reba asked. "I'm supposed to be in the second grade."

"I wanted you and Russ to be in the same grade so you could take care of him," Oda replied. "You're such a smart, good girl and

Russ...well you know how boys are, minds running all over, gettin' into things they shouldn't." Oda nodded. "You tell Miss Smart that you're both coming to the first grade together because I wanted you to. She'll soon find out that you can read and all that but...you just let her know that I said so. Okay?"

"Yes, Momma. I'll take care of him," Reba promised with a sigh. "Besides, my friend Elizabeth is already through the first grade, so I can't catch up with her anyway," she added, philosophically.

On the first day of school that year, Miss Smart divided the kids into classes.

"Now, the first grade will sit on this side of the stove and the second grade will sit on that side." The teacher gestured to opposite sides of the room as she prepared to teach two grades at once, which was no easy task. She had to get things organized right away, so everyone would understand.

The school had four rooms for seven grades: first and second in Miss Smart's room, third and fourth in Miss Jackson's room and fifth and sixth in Mrs. Rudy's room. The seventh grade, which was just five pupils, four of them girls, was taught in the little anteroom off the side of the room for the fifth and six graders, and they worked on their own with oversight by Mrs. Rudy. In 1931, at the depth of the Great Depression, most of the boys had already dropped out of school by the seventh grade to work and help their parents make ends meet.

"Alright," Miss Smart announced in her strongest voice to calm the children down and get their attention. "I want the first graders to stand and introduce themselves so we all get to know each other."

An oversized boy who took up the first two seats on the teacher's right stood up and proclaimed, "I'm Pookey Martin and I didn't get to go to school last year 'cause we moved three times. My daddy cuts trees."

"Thank you, Pookey. And who is sitting next to you?"

Before Pookey could answer (if he was supposed to) the little dark-haired girl jumped to her feet and introduced her self, "I'm Freda and my sister is in the third grade."

"Thank you Freda. I'm sure we'll be hearing from you again." Miss Smart's lips twitched. Then she looked directly at Russell and Reba. "And who do we have here in row two? Are you twins?"

"I'm Reba Gilley," she said, bouncing up. "And this is my baby brother, Russell."

"He is your baby brother?"

"Yes ma'm. Russell, James Russell Gilley," She wanted to get that straight and her momma had told her to make sure that the teacher knew Russ. "I would have thought you were twins. You're both so big for the first grade."

"He's big. I'm almost two-years-older than him."

"You are? Well, why are you just starting the first grade? You're plenty smart. I can already tell that."

Reba swallowed. "Wwwell…well, Mom wanted us to go to school together so we could help one another."

"Sooo, so you could help one another. Hmmmm," Miss Smart repeated. "I'll tell you what, Reba. I want you and Russell to stay behind when we go out to recess. After everyone has had a chance to tell who he or she is, we'll have a little chat. Okay?"

"Yessum," the worried eight-year-old muttered as she sat down to wait for recess and whatever else that might relieve the tension of her first day in school with her baby brother.

"She did what?" Oda exploded later that afternoon as Reba stood there, explaining how she ended up in the second grade even though she'd never gone to first grade.

"I've never heard tell of such. What does Miss Smart know any-way?" Oda exhaled and physically demonstrated her aggravation. "Did you tell her that Ruby and Pearl was in the other room? They could have straightened her out. They knew that I wanted you to be in the same grade with Russ so we could all work together. Now you'll be in other books and Russ, Russ, he'll be on his own."

"Yes, Mom. That's what the teacher said after she asked me to read from the first grade reading book. It's easy. Russ is smart and he'll have fun learning to read that book."

After more than an hour of raging about Miss Smart sticking her nose into family business, Oda relented.

"Oh well, at least you're in the same room and you can walk to school together. That's better than nothing. And you can share the lunch bucket and the pint of cow's milk in the Ball jar."

She nodded as though it was settled to her satisfaction.

"And you'll still have to help Russ with his reading just like Bell and Pearl helped you."

◆   ◆   ◆

Why is he smiling now? The nurse thought as she tended the wounded GI. *What is there to smile about in this desolate place in the midst of all these hospital tents, in this god-forsaken place they call the Ardennes? They just keep bringing boys in here from that Elsenborn Ridge all shot up. Many will die; the rest of them will never be the same. Why is this poor boy smiling? He has to know that with his wounds, he'll never leave Belgium.*

◆   ◆   ◆

Russ wasn't in Belgium. He wasn't even in the Army. He was reliving the first grade back at home in Washington County, Virginia. Miss Smart found things for Reba to do as a teacher's little assistant and Russell discovered he could spread his wings a little with his big sister distracted. He liked recesses best. He could run and play and tire himself out. It wasn't a problem sitting the afternoon out after that playing. Just staying awake was the problem.

He was smiling at how Mom had been thwarted, Reba had been distracted, and he became just another first grader in rural Virginia. He didn't know there was a Depression, because everyone in school looked just like him in their hand-me-down clothes and all.

It was fun, and over the years, as he grew and changed, it stayed fun.

◆   ◆   ◆

As the bloody dawn stained the Belgian sky, the nurse came to him with a long needle dripping with blessed numbness. Russ was glad to get stuck. As he drifted into the deep drug-induced sleep, he remembered how Oda had cried and hugged him after the whipping. Nestled in mom's arms the pain from the switch just slipped away. He was with Mom.

Reba Explains a Fact of Life

"What has he been talking about today?" the doctor asked, coming in out of the wet, snow that blanketed the hospital tent city.

"Well, just listening to one side of the conversation, it seems that Russ is having a serious discussion with Rebe, as he called his sister. It sounds like they're close. Maybe twins," the nurse replied.

Rebe. The name triggered another memory as Russ lay in limbo, not getting better and not getting worse. Feverish and semiconscious, he once again drifted back home, reliving a moment far sweeter than his present state.

◆   ◆   ◆

"I just don't understand Mom at times. Why's she so nervous about me, and what I'm doing and all? Why can't I just be like the other guys on the team?" The big (some thought) overgrown, 16-year-old boy was complaining' to his sister, Reba.

It was a Thursday night in 1940 and they were sitting on the elevated porch of their Eagle Bottom house. The boy rubbed his hands through a thick mop of piss-burnt brown hair. Close to 6 and ½ feet tall and at more than 220 pounds, the Fries High School freshman football tackle was upset because once again his momma had told him no when he wanted to do something. As far as he could tell, she was always telling him no and saying it was for his own good.

Reba, who was 17 years old and tall, herself, tried to console her towering baby brother, even though they both knew things wouldn't change. As far as Momma was concerned, Reba was responsible for Russ. Ever since they'd started school back down in Washington

County, she had been shadowing him. That was the way their mother wanted it, so that's the way it had been.

"Russ, you have to understand Mom. She's scared to death that she's going to lose you like she lost Daddy," she responded.

"Daddy died from pneumonia. She can't stop that, can she?"

"No she can't stop someone from dying after they've gone and caught or done something. How a body dies is not what she's worried about. It's trying to figure out *how* she might lose you that worries her to death."

"Well, she don't want me to drive, and I guess I could get killed in a car wreck," Russ said. "Why is she so worried about football, or going out after the game on Friday for a beer, or maybe going out with some of the cheerleaders? None of that is going to kill me, is it?"

"Well you never know. Remember that Vaughan boy up the river who was doing a hundred miles an hour on 94 and ran head on into those Mormon missionaries? He killed two of his friends and all three of the missionaries. Now, he'll be lucky to ever walk again. He had some beers and was with some girls. See what showing off got him? Mom worries that you'll do something like that and she'll lose you like she lost her momma and daddy. Kids driving crazy around these crooked roads really gets her."

"Wood and Bill dated and then got married and it didn't kill them, did it?" Russ said.

Reba snorted.

"You know they didn't have Mom's permission. Bill just did it before Mom knew what was going on and Wood was just bull-headed as usual and told Mom up front before he did it. She was madder at Wood than she was Bill. She shunned them both for a while, and ignored Forest and Hattie. That is, until little Rex and baby Wade arrived and she wanted to get next to her grandbabies. So she gave in."

"Bet she'll want to control their lives, too," Russ suggested to his sister.

"Nah. She just likes you Gilley boys. Ha!"

"What about Belle and Pearl? They got married and she didn't do anything to them," he grumped.

"Bell had her own mind and Mom thought Henry would take good care of her. Mom always liked Henry. Pearl is just Pearl, well that was something else, you know. Maybe kinda like Mom, don't you know?"

Russ stretched out on the steps and cocked his head at his sister.

"Not that I'm considerin' it any time soon, but why's she so against marriage?"

"It's because she had such a hard time. Her momma died right after her sister was born. She and her brother had to live with our grandpa for a while."

"How long did she live with him?"

"Well, when granddaddy remarried he didn't have room for Mom so she grew up with the Davis family."

Reba shook her head, like one mature woman sympathizing with the life of another.

"Then when she *did* get married, she was twenty-four-years-old and could take care of herself. Daddy was a big guy, like you and Wood, and she thought he could take care of things."

"He did, didn't he?" Russ asked. He had great memories of his big, strong father.

"He did take care of her."

"Yeah. At first it was great. Then she had seven babies in ten years—and no twins either. They moved around a lot before the Depression came along and things got real hard. Then Daddy up and died from pneumonia."

"I remember him down at the Hospital in Abingdon."

Russ remembered being terrified by that place and by the look on his momma's face when she told him that daddy was going to the "promised land."

"But you don't know how worried she was or what bad shape we all were in," Reba said. "There she was with seven kids to feed. You were just ten then, just a baby, and she had no prospects of a normal life.

How could she not worry about something like that happening to us and especially you—the baby?"

"Rebe, you gotta understand. I gotta live my life just like she did. She can't stop me from doing everything that living is all about, including playing football and liking the cheerleaders. She won't even trust me to do the little things."

"Well she likes to know everything, you know that. For Mom to accept something, it has to be her idea. Her plan, you know."

Reba crossed her arms and gave Russ a mock stern look, but with her characteristic twinkle in the eye.

"And when you bark back at her, like tonight at supper, I don't blame her for being upset. If you were mine, I'd have chewed your ass out, too."

"Well just you remember. You don't know how embarrassing it was to have you try to go to the first grade with me when you should have been in the second. I remember. Then after the teachers caught on and pushed you up a grade, you still carried my lunch, checking my coat and talking to my teacher about me. I hated it then. You know that? It made me feel so little. Still does. Do you know that? I remember it like it was yesterday."

"I could've guessed. But Mom told me to do it, and I did."

"You always do what she says. Is that the reason you get along with her so good? Is it because you don't argue with her much?"

Reba shook her head with a knowing well beyond her years.

"I don't always agree with mom and I don't always do what she says, but at least I try to give her some room after all she's done for us."

Russ scowled.

"Sometimes Wood is just like her. I asked him if he would let me take his car to a football game over at Rural Retreat the other day and he almost fell off the milk stool. Wood could've spilled all the milk from that rented cow. He told me all sorts of stories about boys he knew running' too fast and wrecking' their cars. He told me about an accident over on Cripple Creek where the guy was doing over a hundred miles an hour when he left the road and sailed in the air way over into the creek. All three of them were killed and Wood told me the driver was only seventeen."

"You see why Mom is worried."

"Yeah, but she's still tighter on me than on you."

"That's your opinion," Reba countered.

"Why's she so worried?" Russ asked, genuinely puzzled.

"She's afraid she'll make a mistake and let you do something she'll regret. It's what she doesn't know that worries her."

"Well she doesn't have to worry, 'cause she'll never agree on anything that would hurt me. I might do it, but not 'cause she agreed to it."

"I hope so," Reba retorted with a knowing look on her young, but serious fair face. "I hope so."

No Fooling Around Allowed

Many times Russ had not stopped to take advice from his mother, Oda, and it had gotten him into trouble.

Now it was big, big trouble.

Whack, whack! The switch crackled through the air and pain ripped through his body like a drill into bone. "Oh! Oh God! Mom, Mom," he yelled. "What in the hell did I do? What did I do?"

◆　　　◆　　　◆

"What did he say?" the medic asked, looking at the nurse in the dimly lit hospital tent. Once again they were pulling a twelve-hour shift as the casualties mounted each day. The Battle of the Bulge saw more than 40,000 casualties, half of whom died. Those who were treated with dispatch often made good recoveries. Others, like Russ, lingered in the half-world between dead and alive.

"Something about his mom?" the medic guessed, trying to interpret the boy's drugged ramblings.

"I don't know," the nurse said. "He's always, always talking to his mom when he's in such pain. I wish we didn't have to give him the morphine or the other drugs, but they're for the best, really. At least he doesn't hurt so much when he goes under."

Pain rippled through Russ's body as the morphine wore off. The sharp pain jogged his memory, bringing forth a dream of his mother giving him one heck of a whipping. He was the love of her life and she doted on him, but there were some things she would not tolerate—no exceptions.

He relived one of those 'exceptions' as he sweated and turned and tossed.

◆   ◆   ◆

It was a November night (or rather early morning) in 1942, and he'd slipped into the house and eased into his bed. Ever since Wood had left home to get married, Russ had his own bed. He lay there, wide awake, wondering whether his mom had heard him. He hoped not, but then the door to his room squeaked and he knew she was there. He could feel her presence. He remained quiet, hoping against hope.

Then the cover was jerked off, leaving his lanky body protected only by jockey shorts and an undershirt. He cringed, knowing what was coming. He had seen Wood get it when he was a teenager.

And boy, did he get it.

*Whack…whack…*the half-inch thick, four-foot long birch whistled as it hit his legs and behind again and again. As was her way, Oda Gilley mixed criticism and advice to her beloved baby boy as she administered punishment.

"Thought you could slip in after midnight and fool me did you? Well you know better and tonight you get a lesson." She laid into him with a vengeance. "Where were you so late? Where, I say? Where? And who was you with?"

Russ heard himself babbling, "Mom, Mom, we just went to Jimmy Atwood's place. You know over in North Carolina. God, that's all, that's all, and that's the truth!! Mom! Just let me explain!"

"Jimmy Atwood's place? You mean that all night beer joint? You mean that damn dance hall and beer joint? So that's where you've been. You know I don't tolerate that. You know I don't."

Yeah, he knew. He'd gone anyway. "Please Mom, please. All the guys go over there. Wood's been there and so has Bill—before they got themselves married," he rambled, pleading for mercy.

Tonight there was none, for his mother had a point to make. Oda Gilley had lost her husband Webb in 1934 when all seven of her children still lived at home with the youngest, Russ, was just ten-years-old. That had taught her one lesson: that getting married and having babies was the sure way to heartbreak and hardship.

She was dead set against her sons dating, and considered it lots worse than having a few beers with the guys. With a mother's sixth sense, she knew that while Russ probably had told the truth about being at Atwood's, he'd been with more than 'the guys.' Though each of Oda's kids broke the no dating rule sooner or later, Russ was her baby. She'd beat 'later' into him if it killed her. She was frightened to death that he would run off and get married or get a girl pregnant and be shackled in poverty for the rest of his life.

"Were you out with that Swanson girl, Betty Ann, the one who works in the mill and lives on Second Street? I know about her. Tell me the truth right now and I mean it. Now!"

"She was there, but we just danced a couple of times."

"She didn't go with you? How about last Saturday night when you came home really late and had trouble getting up the next morning? Pretending to be sick? You were puking and all that. That didn't happen?"

"But, but Mom, Mom," he started a defense, but did not get a chance to finish it.

"I heard about it from your cousin Claire," Oda yelled. "All about last week. How she saw you pick the girl up on Second Street and how you laid down rubber with Wood's car as you went flying out Main Street. It's a wonder that Bruce Smith didn't catch you and put you in the jail for speeding like that. Claire told me how you took her to her grandma's up in Spring Valley where you could slip in late and the poor woman wouldn't know it."

"Mom! Mom! Stop that switch and please let me answer! I'll straighten this out. I'll tell you," Russ pleaded.

Pulling back, exhausted and looking for an excuse to stop, Oda appeared to relent.

"Alright. Then tell me. Tell me your side."

Russ sat up on the edge of the bed.

"Did you know that you might wake Rebe and Rube up?" he whimpered, his head in his hands.

Oda bellowed to clearly make her point, "WAKE REBA AND RUBE UP?" Oda bellowed. "WHAT ARE YOU TALKING ABOUT? This is me and you and now!"

Russ winced.

"I mean let's not be so loud. Let's just you and me talk. Okay?"

"Well, let's get at it. You told me you'd set me straight. So set me straight!"

"Mom, me and Betty Ann are just good friends. That's all. She works hard in the mill to help her momma and sisters and we just wanted to have some fun. She's a good girl."

"Where did you go? What did you do and when did you leave her grandma's house and come home? Remember, you think I'm asleep when I'm not."

"Okay, Okay." Russ accepted the inevitable. "We didn't go to Atwood's tonight 'cause she was too tired."

Oda pounced on that.

"Where did you go then?"

"We went over to Galax and went to the movies. Saw a double feature and then came home."

"Came straight home?"

"Well, no. We stopped at the Riverside Café, you know, where 94 hits into U.S. 58? We had a Coke and a hotdog."

"So you went into the café and ate?"

Russ clenched his teeth and grimaced as his backside still stung. What was she getting at anyway? Why did she have to know every detail?

"Actually, we sat in the car and one of those little girls in the uniforms brought our food out to us. We talked and ate and listened to the radio."

"What else did you do?"

"Well, we drove to old lady Swanson's so Betty could spend the night with her granny."

"Did you go in?"

"Ummm, just to the door to tell Betty good night."

"That was all?"

"Yes. That was all. By then it was late so I started home. Then I saw some guys down at the creek drinking beers so I stopped and had one with them, and then came on home."

Having won the argument, or so he thought, Russ felt like going to sleep. He rolled over hoping his mom would give up and go to bed herself. Then down came the switch on his bare legs, as Oda gave him her side of the conversation.

"Did you know that the other day Betty's Granny was going to the mailbox and found something lying in the creek that shouldn't have been there? Yes you do and you know what it was, *don't you?*"

Oda continued the whipping that Russ thought he had avoided, just as he thought he'd disposed of the evidence to which she referred. His momma was out to make a point and he took his medicine, but he sensed that this was the beginning of a new chapter in their long test of wills.

Wonder What Russ Did Back Home

"Wonder what he did back home?" the medic said while he and the nurse cleaned Russ's wounds for the evening, changed his bandages, and checked whether he needed more morphine, the savior of shell-shocked soldiers.

"Don't know," the nurse said. "He talks about his family a lot in his delirium, but he never talks about working. I wonder, too."

◆   ◆   ◆

Russ barely heard the words, and didn't really understand what they were talking about or who was talking as he drifted back into the world of dreams and remembrances.

◆   ◆   ◆

"Wood, do you think you and Bill could get me a job at the powder plant down in Radford?" Russ whispered into the telephone so his momma, who was standing out on the front porch talking to somebody, wouldn't hear.

"Hell, Russ. We got you the job at the cotton mill and then you claimed you hurt your back. The work down at the powder plant is lots tougher than that."

There was a pause, then the real truth.

"Besides, Mom doesn't want you on the road so much. Down in Dublin we have to live in old crowded boarding houses and it ain't any fun."

"Wood, Goddamn it! You know that those pissing bastards at the mill took it out on me for you and Bill running off to work at Radford. Everybody knows that you guys are making it good. Both of you got newer cars since you went down there."

"Okay," Wood said, standing up. "I gotta go now. I'll stop by and pick you up and we'll talk some more about this. Okay."

"Sure, but I don't know why you just can't do it," Russ said, getting the last word.

◆   ◆   ◆

The horn rang out real loud and Russ looked out the window through the curtains to see Wood sitting in his car smoking one of those Camel cigarettes. Russ bounded out the door yelling over his shoulder.

"Mom, Mom, I'm going to out talk with Wood for a minute."

There they took up where they had left off on the telephone.

"Russ, damn it. Mom needs you in Fries. You all know how Bill is married and Belle is married and living in Smyth County. You know that! Rube is running around with Foy and gonna get married. If you know anything, you know that. Pearl is already married to Doug. You and Reba gotta mind Mom and take care of her. You know. Be here with her. Mom needs you here."

All this talk about what Mom wanted and how he had to think about Mom was irritating Russ. He wanted to break out and get his own car and maybe just, maybe just go live in a boarding house in Dublin like Bill and Wood. He cursed.

"God, do I know that Wood! Everybody tells me again and again. Pearl was on me just last week. I know you and Doug got me that job at the cotton mill, but those bastards they wouldn't let up."

"Hell Russ, you just don't like work. The girls always got you off. Mom would send you to the fields with Rube and Pearl and then they'd buy that tale that your stomach hurt or something like that.

Then when Mom got on your ass, Rube always took up for you. I know all about that. So don't tell me anything."

Russ now looked sheepish and grinned a little as he listened to his older brother, the guy who had in some ways replaced his father almost a decade earlier.

"Wood, would you just try for me?" Russ asked in a quiet voice. "Please? I won't ask another favor if you will help me this time."

"Okay, but I have to let mom know. Russ, she is worried about you all the time. Sure I know she worries about all of us and she wants to be sure things go right. Sometimes what she thinks is right is not what we think, but she's had hard and frightening times all her life. She's worried about is and she's especially worried about you. Somehow, because you were the baby and Daddy really liked you she feels that she owes it to him to really take care of you."

"God, Wood. I know she does, but she is so rough about how she does it and what she says. Did she ever talk to you like that?"

"Yeh, but not when I was your age because she always depended on me to help with the others." Wood replied.

"Mom has a soft heart you know. When we were in Washington County during the depression she would feed just about any stray guy that came wandering along with his belongings in a beat up suitcase. Daddy would fuss at her saying we were barely footin' the bill for ourselves much less every tramp that came down the road. It was her soft side showing."

"Why did she do it if daddy said not to? Russ asked.

"She thought that maybe, just maybe, God would pay her back and somebody would feed Bill if he needed it."

"Was that when Bill ran away?"

"Yeh. Bill just wanted to be on his own and soon as he was able, he hit the road. First he went to West Virginia near a place called Logan, and got a job as a water boy in a coal mine. It was hard and dangerous so he jumped on a train (a hobo) and went west. We never knew for sure where Bill was, but he was for sure gone."

"She never heard from him?"

"No. None of us did until he showed back up. He was a mess and he was glad to be home again."

"So mom fed tramps that showed up praying that somebody somewhere would feed her boy?"

"Yep. That's what she wanted and I think she was praying for Bill. She does pray for all of us you know. Especially since daddy is gone. She's trying to do everything she wished he would have done and everything she should have done. Sometimes Mom over does it, but just you remember, she does it out of love even when it doesn't seem like it."

"Okay, Wood. I understand, but it doesn't make anything easy."

"I know. I know, Russ," Wood said, sadly all the while puffing on his cigarette and looking out into the night sky. "I know."

"Then you'll do it?" Russ returned to his main question about getting him a job at the powder plant.

"Okay, okay Russ. I'll talk to mom and Bill and we'll try. We'll try."

Wood knew all the while that he was giving in again.

◆   ◆   ◆

A few months later the same two Gilley boys got together at the Riverside Café between Galax and Fries on the New River. Wood had left the powder plant to work for the railroad as a fireman and was *not* pleased to hear that, once again, Russ didn't like the job his brothers had gotten for him.

"Damn it, Russ! You can't just quit," he shouted, as they sipped bottled Cokes.

"It'll make me and Bill look bad. We put our ass on the line for you down at the Hercules Plant. You and me talked about this last year when you wanted to quit the cotton mill and work at the powder plant. You promised this was it and you wouldn't up and quit. Now you want to quit and go into the Army? Come on. You can't do that to Mom!"

Russ was filling out and looking more like the man his brother Wood was. He was over 6 feet 4 inches tall and weighed 230 pounds. His rich brown hair was grown out more than his brother's and slicked back most of the time, as his momma had always encouraged him to look neat and well groomed. She thought he was handsome and enjoyed seeing him dressed up, but not when the girls came around.

Russ was a good-natured boy out for a good time that seemed to his siblings to be all the time. He couldn't seem to concentrate on more than one thing at any given moment. This had made school troublesome, or as Principal Woodson said, "Problematic" for him. He tried to balance book learning with taking directions from the teachers and then offset all that against his interests in the older girls in the one room school and the temptations offered by his cousins and male friends.

Now he was finding he couldn't make himself focus on work, which made it hard to keep a job after he dropped out of school. He liked having money that his mom didn't always keep account of, and having his own car was special. No more borrowing or trying to borrow his big brother's car. Wood was so damned cranky about who drove his car. It was just too hard to keep all those balls in the air. So sometimes work had to give.

Russ had an infectious crooked smile that usually got him his way with family and with girls. He tried it on for size, hoping to soothe his brother.

"But Wood, all the guys I know are going to fight the Germans and Japs. How can I just stay at home, run around in my car, and be petted by Mom? You all say I'm petted. I need to go out and prove that I'm a man, not Mom's baby for life."

Wood's face turned red. He had tried and tried to make the boy understand the facts of life. He just couldn't seem to get anything through Russ's hard head.

"One thing you need to get straight, boy," he said, raising his voice. "You'll always be Mom's baby, no matter what! That's a fact of life you need to live with. It don't matter whether you join the Army or not."

"Wood, why is Mom so against me going to war? It looks like most everybody is doing it and they ain't stopping because they got a good job at the powder plant. Not that it's such a goddamn good job," he said, lowering his voice on the last part.

"Russ, you have to understand that ever since Dad died, Mom has been running scared. She don't want nobody to get married and she sure don't want to lose you or see you come back from the war like Dad's brother, Charles."

"What was the story on Uncle Charles again? I know he died and I've heard it, but guess I don't listen so carefully."

"Well, he had two kids, but wanted to fight the Germans so he up and volunteered for the Army in 1916 and was sent to France and Belgium. He spent a whole winter in the trenches freezing in the mud, looking across barbed wire at the German lines. Then there was this battle and the Germans shot canisters of mustard gas at the Americans. Then the canisters fell short and the wind blew the gas straight at Uncle Charles and he breathed it. They treated him in a hospital in Belgium and then sent him home."

"So he came home alive?" Russ asked, thinking this proved his point.

"Yeah, but he was never the same. He was in and out of hospitals the rest of his life and died of breathing problems in '24, the year you were born. He'd been sick and couldn't work for over six years before he just gave up and died."

Wood paused looking into the distance, hoping to change the subject. He had learned that you could sometimes avoid awkward conversations by changing the subject on Russ.

"I was named for him, you know."

Woodrow had been named for President Woodrow Wilson because when he was born the country was doing well and everybody admired the president. His popularity wore thin with most Americans later on because of his actions abroad, involving American boys in World War I. For the next three elections the country elected Republicans even though they were not that good. Oda turned against Wilson, too, as did most of the Gilleys.

"Mom would have changed my name if she could," Wood continued. "Wilson wanted to make the world do right, but he started the war that killed Uncle Charles."

"But you went to court and had your name changed from Charles Woodrow to Woodrow Charles Gilley."

"Well everybody called me Woodrow or Wood so I just thought it should be first. It had nothing to do with Woodrow Wilson or any of that stuff about Uncle Charles and World War I. Dad wasn't much of a Wilson fan anyway. It was Mom who liked him so much."

"Think I'll go over to Independence and have my name changed around, too. I'm James Russell Gilley, but everyone calls me Russ. It doesn't make much sense anyway."

"You're named for Pop, as you well know. And Wade is named for daddy, too—James Wade Gilley. Forest calls him Wade, though. We've all got the same deal. They name us and then call us by our middle name. Mom wanted me to name Wade for Pop and Forest insisted that we call him Wade. My daddy wanted to name me for his father and his brother Charles and Mom wanted to name me for Woodrow Wilson. Don't make much difference, though. We are who we are."

"Wood, I'm serious about this," Russ pleaded, getting back to the subject at hand.

"About what, Russ?"

"I'm going to change my name around and then join the Army."

"Well it's going to be easier to change your name. You're under age and Mom has to sign for you to enlist."

"I know, I know, but she will. Don't you think?"

"Russ, please, don't you even ask her. Mom has been through so much and she is so afraid to think about losing even more. She is scared to death that Pearl's Doug or that Ruby's Foy will be killed. Then they will end up like her with no husband to help. If she had any inkling that you might get in early she'd be fit to be tied. You know that she don't want you to go."

"But Wood, Mom has to know that we have to live our own lives. Don't she?"

◆   ◆   ◆

Half conscious in an army hospital, far from the Blue Ridge Mountains and his momma, Russ smiled as he thought of his older brother, Wood. Their daddy died when Wood was just a senior in high school. Wood had to grow up fast, and that meant giving up his hopes of a basketball scholarship. Whatever happened, he'd always been there for Russ. Wood was like a daddy, but still a brother. People thought that Russ and Wood were a lot alike. They were both tall and athletic, both hardheaded like their mom, or so their sisters claimed. There was one big difference, though. Where Mom never seemed to give in to Wood or Bill, and while she seemed to want to dominate Russ, in the end she always gave in and let him do what he wanted.

That was both good and bad.

Giving in Again

"Who's that carrying on?" the doctor asked as he joined the incoming shift at the field hospital in Belgium. It was January 1945. "I heard him talking out of his head before I even came in the room.

"It's our boy, Russ," the nurse said. "He's been visiting Fries again, and this time he and his momma are going at it."

"What do you think he's dreaming about now? Sounds like he's telling his mom she was right."

"Every time he comes out from under the morphine, he starts talking to somebody, and he's talking to his mom today. I think she's put her foot down about something."

The tired nurse paused and looked around the hospital tent and the rows of healing and dying.

"It sounds to me like he should have minded his momma on this one," she said quietly.

◆　　　◆　　　◆

"Mom, why? Why did you do it?"

It was early in 1944. Russ and his mother sat bundled up on the front porch. Down by the creek in Eagle bottom, the whippoorwills cried from the bushes.

"Russ, I just couldn't let you do that and live with myself. Just couldn't do it. I just couldn't let you go off and get killed when I knew you had forged my name. I just could not let it happen that way."

"I was halfway through Basic and you made them boot me out! God, Mom! Do you know how embarrassing that was? Everybody at the base hollered and whooped as I left. Then when people on the bus

34

asked me where I was going what could I tell them? 'Going home to momma.'"

Russ wiped his eyes and drew sympathy from his mother. She felt relieved and regretful at the same time.

"Don't blame me. You were the one who forged my name on the application. Why'd you go and do that?"

"God, I couldn't have asked you 'cause you'd have hollered no and then given me a lecture about Uncle Charles running off to France in the last war and what that did to his family. I don't have a family, no kids to worry about. Besides you won't let me even think about marriage."

Oda nodded.

"Right, right and I meant it. You don't need to be married at your age and you don't need to be over there fightin' no war. You're not old enough to do either."

Oda seemed to be against matrimony even though it had been her dream until she met Webb. She had seen so many of her kin jump into marriage early and fall into deep poverty during the Great Depression years. She married her 21-year-old husband when she was 24, and then wound up a tenant farmer's widow with no prospects for feeding and raising their seven children.

In the minds of some (especially the women her first two sons married), Oda became obsessed with her belief that marriage was a sure path to hard times. Perhaps, they argued, she'd had so much freedom before her marriage that she'd seen it as prison once she was behind the bars of marriage and motherhood, then widowhood.

Frustrated, Russ shoved his hands through his hair.

"God, do I ever know that I'm not old enough. You got me booted out of Basic, and here I'm home—no service pay, no job, no gas, and no car. I'm just sitting around here on your front porch thinking about Foy and Doug, or about my friends Fred and Joey and all the other guys who are just about finishing boot camp. How in the hell am I going to explain this to anybody?"

Oda swatted at him.

"Don't you use the Lord's name in vain! You need to be thanking Him that you got a family that loves you!"

At that, Russ began to cry. His eyes got red, a sight Oda could not stand.

"What are my buddies going to think?" he said.

Oda was obviously bothered as she watched her baby boy. No matter how old or how big, he was her baby.

She remembered how Russ had always been so sensitive to what people thought of him and about him. When the family first moved to Fries and rented the house on Second Street, people soon started calling him Little Gilley because even though he was taller and bigger than anybody his age, he stood in the shadow of his big brother, Wood, who was the tallest guy in town and played basketball on the traveling Y team. Even after Russ grew to Wood's height, people sometimes forgot and called him "Little Gilley," leaving him feeling insecure.

Oda knew it was more than that, though. Several of the men in her family had emotional problems and ended up living off and on with their parents even after they had grown up and married. Wood always recalled that several of the Hilltown boys, relatives of his wife Forest Hill, had troubles with feeling down. Some of them learned to drown their emotions in alcohol and others just weren't right in the head.

Some folk claimed it was due to inbreeding among the Scots-Irish who settled the remote areas of the western Virginia Mountains. Oda didn't think that was so, but those hillbillies did have a funny way of talking that some attributed to the Scots-Irish.

Still, that was neither here nor there, even though she sometimes wondered whether Russ could have some of those problems. He was so unlike his older, self-sufficient brothers or even his daddy. It seemed to come from her side of the family. That was why she was always focusing on him and what he did and the decisions he made.

Over the years, he'd gotten to where he knew what she was going to say before she started. It was like they could read each other's minds.

"Russ, you're mad now, but in time you'll appreciate what I did. I probably saved your life.

"I've been mad, too," she said, staring off into the starlit night. "I've always been mad at my daddy for not taking me with him when he remarried that ass of a wife."

She stood and stretched, and thought, *I get mad at my momma for dying and leaving me to fend for myself and depend on relatives like Uncle Ed.* She glanced back down at Russ, hoping they were done, that he'd go sulk off his mad spell and get over it.

God, she thought, *give me the strength to hold on and say no. He'll get over it in a few days. He always does if I hold out. But it's hard.*

"Damn right I'm mad!" Russ said. Tears welling in his eyes, he jumped up and stomped into his room. Out through the screen door Reba came looking back over her shoulder at the disappearing Russ. Like Rube and Pearl, she was prepared to take Russ' side, as usual.

"Mom, what are you going to do?" Reba asked. "He's taking this hard. It'll stay with him forever."

"I know, I know," Oda mumbled, thinking to herself, *I know whatever happens, it'll be my fault. I struggled with this boy forever it seems and I never get it right. What would Webb want me to do? Webb, this boy is more like you than I can stand. I want you to know you left me with a real problem, a boy I love with all that's in me but he's hard, so hard to deal with. He's hardheaded, and you might think that's from me, but you were a knucklehead, too. What am I to do? What am I to do?*

"What did Pearl say?" Reba interrupted Oda's thoughts with a touch. The two women had developed a symbiotic, special relationship that would last them the rest of their lives.

"She thinks I'm right. She sure doesn't want her brother to end up in a hospital like her husband's shell-shocked brother. Pearl always tried to get me to be soft on Russ, but this time she agrees. He ain't got no business over there in Europe."

"What about Rube?"

"Rube is worrying about her Foy over there in France just like Charles was. But she always takes Russ's side. 'Let him do what he wants to,' that's what Rube always says. 'He's got to grow up sometime.'" Oda snorted. "She's no help."

Mother and daughter talked well into the night until Reba finally yawned, excused herself and went inside. Oda stayed on the porch, staring out into the darkness wondering *what is right. How can I make this decision all alone, by myself? Webb, if only you were here to help.*

The next morning Russ woke to the smell of gravy, fatback, eggs, and fresh biscuits. He jumped up, jerked his clothes on and ambled into the kitchen to see his mother at the stove doing what she did best—taking care of her family, cooking the biggest breakfast he had seen in a long time. He sure didn't feel like eating all that. He'd spent the night turning and tossing, mad and worried. His momma had really thrown up a roadblock this time.

Then again, she was cooking too much. Maybe that meant something was up.

"What's this for, Mom?" Russ asked as he walked into the kitchen and stood beside her near the wood-burning cook stove.

"Bill and Wood are coming over to have breakfast this morning and I just wanted my three boys to have enough," Oda said.

"What are they doing coming over here? Bill's living in Pulaski, but he says he's going to Oregon and work in an oil plant out there. He ain't got the time to be fooling around here. And Wood is working for the N & W now and he's got Forest and little Wade in Roanoke."

"I went over to Rube's last night and called them. They're coming over this morning. I want to talk to all of you."

"Talk to all of us?" Russ asked, all the while thinking, *what in the hell is she up to now? Why do we need everybody to figure out a simple thing?*

"Yep. I need some help decidin' what's right. I was figuring 'bout it last night and I know what I want to do, I need the family's support." *God I wish Webb was here,* she thought.

The family trickled in, each with a sense that something was up or something was wrong. Oda fed them a large breakfast of what they all enjoyed best, particularly Russ. Then she took her three sons into the sittin' room and closed the doors. She and the girls had talked it to death. Now she had to get the boys to understand.

Bill jumped in as soon as the door was closed.

"Damn it, Mom. Russ's right. He ain't a baby no more."

Just as though he hadn't spoken, because some thought she and Bill were too much alike to gee and haw, Oda turned to Woodrow. He was the "man of the family."

"Woodrow, what do you think?"

They talked for almost two hours, and in the end they came to an agreement. They would give in to baby Russ. Though it pained her to no end Oda was doing it in part because she had become accustomed to giving in by now. It was the easy way out.

Grim faced, she opened the door. The girls took one look at her and knew what had been decided. They hugged each other and shed a tear while Russ grinned.

He was back in the Army.

◆   ◆   ◆

In that hospital bed in Belgium, he wasn't grinning one little bit. He remembered that joining the Army had been the thing to do back there a year ago, and it had been kind of fun for a while. Things had changed on December 16 when the Germans launched their surprise attack, their last desperate gamble. Many of his friends had died. It had been hell.

Now, three days into his agony and with no change in his condition, Russ had to admit, during those moments when he could think clearly, that Mom had been right. If only he could have the chance to tell her. That would set things right.

Russ at Home One Last Time

"Wade boy, I'm doing it for you. Uncle Charles and his friends did it for us and I'm doing it for you and Toodie and Rex and everybody."

◆   ◆   ◆

"What did he say? Who is Wade?" the medic asked.

"Just reliving another moment back home with his family I guess," the nurse answered as they prepared to put Russ back on the makeshift surgical table. She thought to herself *we have to get that stuff out of his lungs if he's ever going to have a chance.* This would be their third major surgical effort to clean out the wound in his side and move his status from critical to serious.

So far there had been little improvement.

The Germans were being beaten back and the critical time was over. The Allied medical corps was pulling out all the stops to save the lives of soldiers wounded in a bloody battle where 20,000 American boys lost their lives and another 80,000 were wounded. They had never seen such a slaughter of soldiers before and it was getting worse as the fighting intensified.

◆   ◆   ◆

"Wade, come here and sit by me on the porch steps," Russ called to his five-year-old nephew. He patted the porch floor with his left hand. A Camel cigarette dangled from the fingers of his right. "I'm headin' out tomorrow and just wanted to say goodbye to you." When Wade sat and didn't say a word, Russ continued, "Now that I'm finally out of boot camp, tomorrow I'll head out to join a brand new division and ship to England. Maybe I'll get to fight those Germans after all."

The little boy did not respond, for his uncle's words were beyond his years.

"It sure is hot in Rube's house with everybody coming to supper to say goodbye, huh?" Russ continued. He kept on talking, not really caring that his nephew didn't understand more than every fifth word. It was better that way, since there was no way in hell Russ would bare his soul to his sisters or brothers, and certainly not to his mother. He thought to himself, *after all the fighting and fussing, I can never admit that I'm wondering if she was right all along. Now I'm leaving her and everybody here going away—over there—where Uncle Charles lost his chance at life in the fields of Belgium.*

He was a little doubtful and a little scared, and he was finding that this, his last night home before heading to Boston to meet up with the 99th Army Division, was harder than he'd ever thought it would be.

"Supper's ready," Oda announced from the screen door.

She directed them like a well-trained drill sergeant.

"Russ will go first, then Wood and then us women."

Bill and Hattie had already left for Oregon—a long way away. Oda might have called Bill hardheaded, others might have concluded, "Like mother, like son."

So she made do with the family she had near, and had done what she did best, cooked up a meal that none of her kids or grandkids would forget—not ever in their lives. She had killed a chicken, or rather Wood had "wrung its neck off," and she'd scalded that big Dominic Rooster, scraped the loosened feathers off, and used it to make the best chicken and dumplings anywhere, anytime. She had also opened a half-gallon jar of canned pork loin and used the grease to make Russ's favorite gravy. The oversized biscuits, canned green beans, and mashed potatoes were what he would remember best of all in the dark days that were to come.

After dinner, she passed a box around the living room so that each person could choose a candy bar for dessert. Wartime meant sugar rationing, so it was difficult for her to make her favorite desserts, and store-bought sweets were almost unheard of for most families. And Russ had been sending her his candy allocation from the Army for months and she'd stored the treats for special events. Everyone was anxious to have his or her turn at Oda's candy box, especially little Wade.

After dinner, Russ leaned on the doorframe between the kitchen and Rube's living room, and smoked his ever-present Camel cigarette as the after dinner conversation flowed around him. The family knew he would be gone for a long time, if not forever. They had heard so much about Uncle Charles and his difficulties in the Fields of Flanders that it made them scared to think of anyone else going across the ocean to France to perhaps lose their lives. "Russ, how come you volunteered to go to cooking school out in Fort Hood, Texas?" Pearl asked. "Never knew you took to kitchen work much."

His older sister had always been a direct talker.

"Huh. If you had your choice of corps medic assistant, latrine cleaner, truck driver, or cook, what would you do?" Russ said, with a snort. "Who else knows where all the food is and how to get first dibs when something special comes in—like, like turkey for Thanksgiving?"

The assembled Gilley clan nodded, smiled, and chuckled. Most of them were tall and, coming out of Hoover's Depression, almost always hungry. They understood Russ and eating.

"What are you going to do in Boston?" Rube asked.

"Join my division. They're puttin' together a whole new army division, the 99th, and people are coming from all across the country. At least that's what Sarge Smith told us. He said the division would be made up of a lot of green kids just like us."

"Green kids?" Wood asked.

"Yeah. Farm boys, hillbillies, like me, and some of those college boys who thought they were going to be pilots or officers, but the

Army decided that they needed more GIs than pilots. Sarge says that with the air power being so good, the main fighting will be on the ground from now on."

Suddenly he was aware of increased tension in the room.

"I'm excited about going over there," he said, with a casual shrug.

"When you get to Boston what will you do?" Wood asked.

Russ replied with a small grin. "We'll wait," he answered, smiling. "The Army is mostly hurry up and wait."

He took a drag on his Camel.

"We'll get to know each other and our outfits, and get ready tgo overseas. I heard there would be a thousand GIs on each ship, and more than thirty ships, not counting the escorts and all that stuff. When we get to England, they say that we'll have a lot of advanced training to get ready for the front lines."

He paused for a moment, and then continued with mixed emotions.

"If we go to the front lines. The others may be in Berlin before we get a chance to get into any fighting."

"I sure hope Ike marches into Berlin long before then," Oda spoke up, thinking it would be better for everybody if Russ never saw the front. She loved talking with her boys. It was like the days when she and Webb were first married. They would sit on the porch and talk and dream (and pray) for all sorts of things. What they got were seven kids, a depression and then Webb died on her. Still, she loved it when she could get in a conversation with the boys. She and the girls talked all the time, however, the boys seemed to go on the defensive when she spoke up too quickly.

Even with all the worry about Russ going overseas, it still was a nice evening there talking with Russ and Wood for they both seemed more grown up than ever before. When the conversation died down some time later, Wood pulled out his old Kodak camera and organized the family for a picture.

◆   ◆   ◆

"Come over here girls and stand with Russ on the steps. Russ, you're tall so you stand on the ground. Mom, you stand on the first step on Russ's left side and Rebe will stand to his left. Rube you and Pearl can stand in back of them."

This was an important picture for everyone was dreading the next few months.

Just as he got everything organized, Forest pushed him aside and took charge.

"Woodrow. You get in there and I'll take the picture. That way everybody who's here will be in it. The whole family, what of it that's here tonight."

She was the only one who didn't call Oda's oldest by his nickname, but she could do that. She was his wife.

After the first shot was taken, she asked Russ to stand with Wade for a minute so she would take a picture of the two of them. The camera clicked, and the moment was frozen in time.

◆   ◆   ◆

To Russ, lying in his bed after the third round of surgery wads reliving that last night at home with Mom and his family at Rube's for dinner seemed so long ago, though it had been just eight months. It had been a real goodbye. Was it a last goodbye? Would he ever get back to Eagle Bottom and Mom's cooking? He could almost taste those chicken and dumplings as he drifted...drifted. And slept.

A Quiet Night

"What did he say?" the medic asked the nurse.

"He's here," she said.

"Here?"

"Yes. He's back in the army. It sounds like he's reliving a night here in Belgium with fellow soldiers."

Russ had moved from memories of home. The nurse sighed as she smoothed a hand across his brow.

"At least he doesn't seem to be hurting."

◆   ◆   ◆

It was November 1944.

Russ remembered it being quiet.

It was very quiet.

So quiet the hidden soldiers could hear the gentle snowflakes float down through the towering evergreen trees. They could almost hear the flakes hit the ground, which was bare around the trees, with snowy mounds covering bumps in the forest terrain. It was dreamlike, a landscape fitting for a Christmas card, and it made the GIs long for home. It made one boy GI in particular long for the Virginia Blue Ridge.

That Sunday evening after Thanksgiving it was quiet and cold. There was little to do. The Germans across the border were hunkered down in their warm wool coats. The American boys in their scant clothing spent most of the time keeping warm as best they could. They thought it strange that America's great industrial machinery couldn't equip her soldiers. They could see the Germans across the front lines appeared well clothed and well equipped, even though their homeland had been intensively bombed for months. Still, the young GIs couldn't do anything about that. So they scrunched up tight and tried to keep warm in their foxholes.

Russ had dug his temporary foxhole when orders came down for his part of the 99th to stop and dig in—they thought for the entire winter. He dug down almost four feet into the frozen Belgian forest floor and squared out the bottom to make more room. Then with a huge farm boy from Indiana, Frank "Jughead" Mitchell, Russ cut and carried pine saplings from the forest and built a roof for their 'hole. Then they covered it with pine boughs for more protection from the elements. The dirt floor was padded with pine needles and wood scraps. They left small holes at either end of the structure, one for watching the distant ridge through the underbrush—or for Germans, as unlikely as the generals thought that was—and the other to scoot in and out and let smoke out if they dared to build a small fire.

Days later, Russ, relatively warm in his thin uniform, snug sleeping bag and a woolen cap pulled down so that only his eyes were visible, looked out over the snow-covered pine needles. He was surprised to see a crouched human figure scrambling across the landscape, head up, looking this way and that as he zigzagged to Russ' foxhole. He wondered *who that could be. Where is he going? Had he lost his mind running around out there in the open?*

Moments later, the small figure reached the 'hole and slipped inside headfirst. It was Charlie, "Squirrel" Hill of West Virginia.

"Thought you might need a cigarette, Russ boy," he said, smiling broadly.

Russ grinned and quickly sat up, letting in a bit of the cold but not noticing now.

"A cigarette? You're damned right! Give me one! Damned right! It's been days (a slight overstatement, but who was keeping score?) since I had one. My damn nerves are tingling all down to my toes.

"I don't suppose it's a Lucky Strike?" he continued, wistfully. "Haven't had a 'Strike' in a long time."

Hill unbuttoned his jacket and pulled out a crumpled pack of cigarettes bearing the Camel logo.

"Nope, you're going to have to make do with these."

"Damn the brand, I need a smoke bad!"

Russ was glad for an American cigarette of any make. He grabbed two before the smaller figure could pull them back.

Squirrel took a smoke for himself, too, and placed the pack secure back inside his jacket. He produced a match, struck it on his leather shoe side (the soles were wet), lit his cigarette, and took a deep breath, inhaling the smoke and then slowing blowing it out. "Need a light?" he said, leaning over toward Russ, his hands shielding the sputtering match.

"Yeah, thanks."

"Where's Jug?"

"Oh, hell. Don't you know? He went to get another one of those damn paperbacks. The guy pulls a book out of his hip pocket and reads while pissing. If he weren't so big I'd call him a 'bookworm.' He'll slide back in here in a bit."

They hunkered back against the dirt, pulled their coats high around their necks, and drew long and deep on their cigarettes, each holding the smoke in his lungs as long as possible before blowing it out. It was like they were back home, sitting among the trees in Wayne or Carroll County, waiting for a deer to wander past and offer itself as added meat for the dinner table. The nicotine was doing its thing, calming them and taking off the rough edges. "Say, Russ," Squirrel said, after a few minutes. "That sure was a little doe you shot on Thanksgiving."

"You sure didn't complain when you were gnawing on those bones the last two nights," Russ replied.

"Nah, it was good. Damned good. A lot better than that cold stuff in tin cans the Army serves us dogfaces. I just kind of hated to kill a momma deer. That's all." Charlie continued.

"Look at it this way," Russ said. "If we hadn't killed it, somebody else in the 99th would have had deer steak these last two days instead of us hillbillies. Hell, even the Whiz Kids would have done it, if they knew how." He laughed.

"And those Germans would have enjoyed the meat if that little momma had wandered over there, too. So let's not be complaining' about having' a good meal or a good time."

"Boy, you sure do admire that brother of yours." Charlie said, suddenly changing the subject.

Russ looked over, through the smoke, for the longest time.

"What? What did you say about Wood?" He demanded.

"I said you miss your big brother. He was a friend as well as being a brother, wasn't he?"

"Well, now that you mention it," Russ mused, "he was a friend, but I never realized it 'til I got over here. He was always on me it seemed, but now I know he was thinking about me, not himself. Wood would give you the shirt off his back. Mom said that was one of his problems— too much worrying about others and not enough about himself—or her was what she meant, I guess."

"He stepped right in when your daddy died?"

"Yeah. Me and Rebe and Rube thought he wanted to run everything. Now I see that he was trying to step in for Daddy. God, somebody had to stop Mom from running every damn little thing. She was frantic sometimes."

"Wood meant well. Yes, he did."

"But he kept coming back to the bird hunting and stuff like that, didn't he?"

Russ took another long draw on the Camel and remembered out loud, "Wood was best at shooting birds on the fly. He'd never shoot them on the ground. Once we were out with his dog, Queenie, and she pointed a big grouse in a pine field. The old bird looked and looked at us, with his head craned up all sharp wondering what we were up to. I shot him dead before Queenie flushed him out. The next thing I knew, Wood whacked me across the back with the butt of his shotgun and knocked me flat on my face in the field dirt. 'Damn you, Russ!' he barked. 'You got to give the bird a chance. Don't you know anything about bird hunting?'"

"Then he pulled me up and brushed me off. 'I won't tell Mom about this if you don't.' he said. He was just trying to teach me a lesson. He always tried. Sure wish I had listened to him more. Sure do wish that now."

"Russ, how in the hell did we end up here at the end of the earth?" Charlie asked a moment later.

Russ took a long drag and blew out another stream of smoke. "I came to fight the Germans. That's what I came for."

"Then they put us here in the hills where Ike thinks there won't be any fighting. The Captain told everybody so!" Russ continued.

"Yeah, but these Belgians aren't so sure he's right. Didn't you hear what Frank overheard? I guess he studied some French in high school, then in college, too. So he can understand these Belgians a little and even tries to talk to them at times. Damned if I can tell what he's saying or if they understand him, though…all gibberish to me."

The French-speaking Belgians were friendly enough with their liberators; however, the language barrier still made the isolated GIs wary. Still, any report of communication was better than none for the isolated GIs.

"Did he say what he heard?" Charlie asked after a pause.

"The villagers say the Germans always come through this forest on their way to the sea. Have done so for hundreds of years. It's the most direct path to the ocean.

"Who knows? Who cares?" Russ said, with a shrug.

He had no idea where the port of Antwerp was. It was all very strange to him and most of his comrades. He had never even looked at a real map of Europe before the war.

Squirrel took another puff.

"Well, I bet Ike has some guys on his staff that knows some French, too. I'd trust them rather than these farmers."

Russ mused. "Maybe you're right.… Maybe."

Russ had learned from dealing with his brothers and sisters and friends in Fries that one way to avoid confrontation was to neither agree nor disagree. Besides, who knew if those "Frenchies" were telling the truth or not? (The newly arrived GIs rarely distinguished between the Belgians and the French.)

For a long time Russ and Charlie sat looking out of the hole at the ridge across the border where the German lines couldn't quite be seen. Each was deep in thought about things in general, and home and family in particular.

"Squirrel" broke the silence.

"So your momma didn't want you to join up? Is that why you keep talking about all that? Hell, my momma didn't want me to either. In fact, she said isn't no way you're going to go over there and die for Roosevelt. That right?" West Virginia was still a hotbed of Hoover Republicanism and they had been against the war from the beginning.

"Yep, my mom was dead set against it," Russ said.

She was usually dead set against things, he thought, or so it seemed. She'd forbidden him most everything he'd wanted to do as a boy. Rebe always said that after their daddy died, she became afraid of her shadow when it came to her baby boy. *Hell,* Russ thought *if Reba says that's it, then that's it. She knows Mom better than anyone else ever will.*

He thought about his relationship with his momma for several minutes before speaking again. "At first, I bluffed and told her that I had signed up and it was all set. Nothing she could do about it. It was all set, too. What she didn't know that I was too young and needed her approval—that I had signed her name and then signed Wood's as a witness. The Army recruiter in Galax said it was okay. Then I was in, for a little while."

"Only for a while? What the hell happened?"

Charlie had heard parts of this story, but never the whole thing.

"Yeah. Wood found out what I had done and told Mom. Damn did she ever hit the warpath? Mom is part Cherokee, you know, and we always said to each other that in her mad fits she was on the warpath. And she had a few." Russ chuckled on thinking about it.

"What happened when she found out?"

"She got her car out of the garage and had Wood drive her to Galax where she got Dale Cottrell, that damned lawyer there, to draw up papers making the Army send me home right in the middle of basic training."

"Where did you do your boot camp?"

"Down in Mississippi—wet ass, 'Nowhere Mississippi.' It was the damn end of the world, if you ask me. It was hot and sweaty, and there was down there were cotton farms. It was so flat you couldn't tell which direction the sun was coming up from, or anything for that matter. Mostly saw coloreds down there, too. Everywhere you looked there they were and do they have it hard."

"Russ, how long did you stay before your momma yanked you home?"

It occurred to Russ that Charlie was always asking questions about a guy's personal life. Why did he need all the details? It made him tired to talk about details, but he tried to answer anyway.

"I was there five weeks. Then Mom found out I'd forged her name, she really turned up the heat. They sent me home on a bus that went from Memphis to Louisville, then to Cincinnati, Pittsburgh, Roanoke and finally home to Galax where Wood and Forest and their little boy picked me up and took me to Mom's house."

He sighed. Just thinking about it made him tired. He remembered being on the crowded bus, hanging around dirty bus stations for hours and hours with nothing except snacks to eat. All he could do was think about the fact that he wasn't going to fight any Germans after all.

"It took four days to get home and then I had to face Mom. I was worn down good." Russ explained.

"What did she say? What did your momma say?" Charlie was really getting to the point.

"Well," Russ thought out loud. "I went in first and walked straight over and picked her up off the ground and hugged her real good. She just broke down. Just broke down and cried and cried. She just couldn't seem to say anything. Then everything was okay. It was all okay for a little while."

"For a little while?"

"Yeah. I had given up my job at the powder plant in Radford. You know the one Wood and Bill had got for me. Everybody was going to war, and there I was stranded with nothing to do except maybe work in the Fries cotton mill. I could work for maybe twenty cents on the hour and that on the graveyard shift. That is, if they'd even have me."

"So what did you do?"

"Well, my buddy, Ilas Gallimore, and "ol Birddog Jennings had a car, a '39 Ford coupe. Actually, it was Ilas' but you would have thought it was Birddog's the way he acted. We ran all over the countryside looking for something to do.

"Once, we came up U. S. 11 from Roanoke and saw some soldiers hitchhiking to Marion and Bristol. Those boys had just got out of boot camp in North Carolina. They were spouting stuff about how they were going over to Germany to kick Hitler's ass and all that. God that really made me mad, 'cause I wanted to kick his ass, too."

"You stopped and talked to them?"

Charlie was interested in everything and he talked about going to college. He talked like he wanted to be a doctor or something. Russ guessed he might make a good lawyer the way he asked so many questions.

"Yep. Ilas pulled over to the side of the road and we got out and talked past midnight, and would have talked longer 'cept they were kinda anxious to get on home."

"Did you give them a lift?"

"Well, Ilas' car was a two-seater with a rumble seat in the back, so we didn't have much room. Ilas kept fretting about it and saying his tires were low on air and one was almost flat. We got out the tire pump and the jack, but the damn jack was broke."

"Broke? So what did you do then?"

"Well, me and Birddog lifted the car's rear end off the ground so Ilas and the soldiers could put a rock under the axle and take off the wheel. Ilas had patching compound and some patches, so we fixed one tire and put it back on. Then we pumped the other tires way up high and all six of us got on and off we went at about 30 miles an hour."

"How did six of you fit into a two-door coupe with a rumble seat? Didn't the soldiers have their things?"

"They each had a duffle bag."

"How did you do it?"

"Do it?"

"Yeah. How did you get the duffle bags in?"

"Well, me and Birddog stood on the running boards and sometimes pushed with our feet to keep the car going when we came to a hill. We did that all the way from Shawsville to Fort Chiswell, where the soldiers thought they could catch another ride on home. We sat there for a while, but no other cars came by and it was way past midnight. I told Ilas, 'Let's take them on to Wytheville.' Wytheville is at the intersection of 11 and U. S. 21 going south, so there would be more traffic. Ilas agreed and we left them boys at the Greyhound bus station in Wytheville before we turned around and headed for home."

"Did they get home?"

"Sure. They must have."

They paused for a while, and each puffed on another Camel while they looked out at the snowflakes and the quiet forest. This time it was Russ who broke the silence.

"Where you from, Squirrel?" Russ asked, turning the tables some.

"Wayne County."

"Wayne County? Where the hell is that?"

"West Virginia. Down on the Ohio River, just south of Huntington."

"Huntington?"

Russ was curious. All of that seemed a long way off from Fries and Eagle Bottom. He had been to Bluefield over in West Virginia but he had never even heard of Huntington. Where was that?

It turned out that Huntington was a big city by Russ's standards. Around the turn of the century, Colis P. Huntington established the city bearing his name on the Ohio River upstream from Cincinnati to be the terminal end of the Chesapeake and Ohio. By the late 1920s, when the stock market crash ushered in the Great Depression (or Hoover's Depression as it was named after the President everyone blamed), Huntington had become a great city. Colis P. Huntington was not only a railroad magnate. He was also a great industrialist and city planner. He had founded the Newport News Ship Building and Dry Dock Company on the Chesapeake Bay and created a city nearby called Hampton which was something of a sister city to Huntington. Both Hampton and Huntington were known for their broad streets and for the large number of industrial complexes nearby, which were attracted because of the C & O.

"Yeah," Squirrel said, nodding his head and thinking of home, "Huntington's the biggest city in West Virginia, where the C & O Railroad ends at the Ohio River. We live just down the Ohio a little bit from it."

"Why's it called Wayne County?"

"Well, it was named for a warrior just like us—'ol Mad Anthony Wayne. He was a big name for his time."

"Mad Anthony Wayne? Who in the hell is that?" Russ was curious. Even though Russ had gone through the ninth grade at Fries, his knowledge of history was limited, as was the case among many Virginia hillbillies.

"That was what some called him. Story goes that he tried to stir up a revolution. Some folks even say he was mad. You know, crazy like. Lots of folks liked him though. They followed Wayne into battle and they thought enough to name things for him."

Then Charlie turned the conversation back on the other soldier, asking, "Russ, what county are you from?"

"Grayson County, Virginia, that's where I come from. God's country! Carroll County is there, too. Wood and Forest they live in Hilltown, which is in Carroll." Russ told Charlie everything at once.

"Grayson, Grayson that sounds like somebody's name. Who was it named after? What did he do to get a county in Virginia named for him?"

"Damned if I know. Nobody ever asked me that before." Russ snapped.

Because Russ hated to show his ignorance, he changed the subject back to Charlie. "What's it like over in Huntington and Wayne County?"

"You've never been to the Ohio River?" Charlie counters right back.

Russ shook his head. "Nope, I've never been out of the state of Virginia before joining this here god damn Army. Chilhowie, Marion, Fries, Galax, Pulaski and Roanoke–the big City of Roanoke–that was all of the traveling I had ever done before joining up.

Then after a little thought he added, "Well, I did go over the line to North Carolina a lot, mostly for beer and dancing, and that's about all."

He paused again for another long minute and added, "When I went to basic in Mississippi and special school in Texas, I didn't learn much about the places. They were different from the mountains of Virginia. I got to the different army posts mostly by bus, but the long trips were mostly by train. I came all the way to Boston from Fries to meet up with the 99th by train. Got to see a lot of the country from the train window, but I didn't learn much history during those trips."

"Well, Huntington and Wayne County has it all over that country. We got the steamboats on the river, got the glass companies and the nickel plant, which have lots of jobs. And we got a college too."

"A college?"

"Yep, Marshall College."

"So Huntington is in Wayne County and I never heard of neither?"

"No, damn it, Huntington is in Cabell County, but it *is* town for us. It has Roanoke beat hands down."

"How do you know that?"

"Well, that's what the Advertiser, the paper says. So, it must be so."

"Oh, must be then."

There was another long pause as the boys dragged on the very butts of those Camels. Then Squirrel asked, "Russ?"

"Yeah?"

"How did you end up back in the Army?"

"Well, seeing those soldiers just burned me and Birddog up. Those guys from Marion were going to war and fighting for America and all that. Fighting Hitler. It just burned us up. It just made us sick. The next thing I knew, ol' Dog had joined the Marines and was off to boot camp at Paris Island, South Carolina. He did it just as soon as he was old enough. And Ilas was talking about when he would do it. I got so damned mad at Mom. I was ugly to her every morning. Wouldn't get out of bed 'til noon no matter how many times she called. I talked to her real awful. I blamed her 'cause I was 'outta things and all my friends were gone or going to fight."

Russ scowled at the remembered embarrassment of being pulled out of the army by his momma. When he left basic training in Mississippi the guys had laughed at him. All the way home everyone he ran into asked where he was going. He shouldn't have worn that uniform home, but he hadn't had the money to buy any regular clothes. Actually there was so many soldiers coming and going that Russ just walked out with his uniform on without saying goodbye to any of the guys in basic. They never knew what happened to him. He wanted it that way because it would have been embarrassing to just leave like he came with shirt and overalls. He was happy to wear the uniform home but it was hard to answer all those questions.

It had been damned embarrassing to have to lie or constantly change the subject. Then, back at home he thought that everybody, and that meant *everybody*, was laughing at him behind his back. It was especially hard to think that the girls were laughing and that hurt the most. Right before he left, when the word got out that he had first signed up, lots of Fries girls had called and been excited to know a fighting man. Then after he came home, he knew that all those girls could think was *His momma pulled him out. Russ is a momma's boy.*

"She gave in, did she?" Squirrel asked, gesturing around as if to say, *I guess she must have. You're here, aren't you?*

"Yeah, she always did when I put on the pressure. Mom always wanted me to be happy and when she decided to she'd always figure out a way. Next thing I knew, Wood got a new set of papers and Mom signed them. She went to the post office and had them witnessed, too. So all I had to do was take 'em to the recruiter and turn 'em in. Before you could say Jack Frost I was back on the bus to Mississippi and boot camp again."

"The same one?"

"Yeah, the same one except that is was different. It was August and the bugs were everywhere and everyone was in a hurry."

"A cook huh? Why did the army think a 6'4" momma's boy from the Blue Ridge Mountains might make a good cook?" Charlie teased.

"Hell, boy you know as well as I do the Army don't think. It just does like it is supposed to do it. It just does it and I was a cook. A damn good one if I do say so."

"So you went all through that and came all the way here to be a cook?" Charlie never seemed to let up.

"Well who knows? Most think we'll be in Berlin soon and Hitler will be dead and this war will be over."

"Maybe...Maybe...." Russ replied looking out over the snow-covered pines his thoughts drifting back to his momma and all that had happened in a few short months. Shortly, they parted company, each to his own place, when Squirrel took his Camels and zigzagged back to his foxhole. Russ snuggled down in his sleeping bag and dropped into a fitful sleep. There was no real rest, though. No matter what Ike thought, history waited.

It snowed all night, and the Belgian-owned Ardennes Mountains on the German border had never looked more beautiful. They would never look the same again, either.

◆   ◆   ◆

"Goodness, he's been talking all night," the nurse commented as the medic joined her at Russ's bed.

"What's he been talking about, or should I say who?" the young doctor asked.

"He's talking to a soldier named Charlie. He seems to be dreaming more recent stuff, poor boy." The nurse pursed her lips. "He sure is turning and tossing a lot. What do you think of his chances?"

The doctor shook his head as he moved to the next bed over. "Not very good, I'm sorry to say. While he's dreaming there's still hope. This one's done dreaming." He pulled the blanket up over the boy's head a clear indication that he was dead.

Russ continued his half sleep, twisting and turning and calling out to his fellow GIs. They were the closest to him in time now.

December 15, 1944; The Night Before

"Come on in Dogface, oops, I mean Frank," Russ chuckled as his tall, gangly friend from Indiana slid into the 'hole in a contorted but quick effort before sitting up against one side. Dogface was a common nickname for GIs during the war; however, to call a friend dogface was a little of a putdown, so Russ had hastily added his version of an apology.

"God Russ, you've got you shoes off and those wet, holey socks around your neck again!" were the first words out of Jughead's mouth as he looked through the darkened interior of the 'hole at Russ.

"Damn right," Russ retorted. "Damn right, and I'll do it all the time to not get Trench Foot." Russ had his sleeping bag partially wrapped around his feet, which were beet red and crowned with whitish toenails. Trench Foot, a condition produced by prolonged exposure to water, was endemic among the American troops during the cold, damp winter in Belgium. It was also common in the trench warfare of World War I, when soldiers stood, sometimes for hours, in trenches that slopped with a few inches of cold water. The name "Trench Foot" came out of the earlier war.

"You don't want to get it? Why if it gets bad enough it could be a ticket home, you know."

"I know, I know. Scottie Franklin from Fries got out and is on his way home now. But God damn, did you see his feet? They may have to cut 'em off. I sure as hell don't want to cut my feet off just to go home. What the hell would I do then?" Russ raged on. "Set around the house with Mom all the time?" Russ shook his head. He didn't want to get home that way. Anyway, he had just got here after a couple of years trying to go and fight the Germans. Much of that time had been spent arguing with his mother. He sure didn't want to do that the rest of his life.

"Hell, some guys over in 'Yellow' company had been reported to be shooting themselves just to get off the front lines and maybe get sent home." Frank reflected aloud. He glanced out the side of the dugout, looking for anything. It sure was eerie out there.

"Sure, some idiots will do anything to get home," Russ replied. "Not me, buddy! Not me! No way that I'm gonna shoot myself."

Frank squinted at Russ and asked, "Thought you bird hunters were such good shots."

"Not that good." Russ snapped. That wasn't anything to kid about, soldiers messing themselves up for life just to get back home. God, why did they come in the first place? He would just take his chances.

"Okay, okay!" Frank retorted. The conversation fizzled out soon afterward as they snuggled down into their bedrolls to spend another night in the middle of nowhere.

Little did they know that before they woke, Hitler would have launched an all out attack against the dug-in Americans? Few would have guessed that a massive German army would come directly at Elsenborn Ridge right through the Ardennes.

◆   ◆   ◆

"Is he still talking or has he settled down?" the medic asked the nurse.

"Well, he has settled down, but now he is reliving the time the Germans started this god-awful battle," she said.

"Poor kid…."

◆　　◆　　◆

The GIs dozed fitfully in the cold and damp. Then the morning came with a fiery sky that was nothing like they had ever seen. It was an all-out assault by the carefully assembled German army, made up of more than 600,000 men. Mortars and 88s literally rained down on American positions, creating death and destruction everywhere. And, as much as anything, it caused confusion and fear.

The company that contained Russ, Frank, Charlie and the others was devastated by the onslaught. Their captain was killed immediately, and the company lost almost half its personnel in the first hours of the onslaught. But the 99th held to fight another day. They held even with devastating losses as the Germans moved on, essentially bypassing Elsenborn Ridge, and some GIs breathed sighs of relief—but not for long.

Little did they realize that same enemy would later turn back and attempt to take Elsenborn Ridge?

◆　　◆　　◆

Professor Stephen Ambrose, the preeminent WWII historian in the U.S., wrote an article on the Battle of Bulge for the Military History Quarterly in which he stated:

> "...to the north, between Monschau and Losheim, the U.S.99th Inf. Div., newly arrived in Europe, and the 2nd Inf. Div....did not simply delay the German advance but stopped it along the critical point of the whole battle, Elsenborn Ridge. The low ridge...was the main objective of Sepp Dietrich's 6th Panzer Army.
>
> Elsenborn (Ridge) was the Little Round Top of the battle. Dietrich drove his units mercilessly, but he could not take it. In the vast literature of the Battle of the Bulge, Elsenborn Ridge always yields pride of place to the far more famous action...at Bastogne. Everyone knows

about the 101st Airborne at Bastogne; almost no one knows even the names of the 99th and 2nd Infantries.

Yet it was along Elsenborn Ridge…that these two ordinary infantry divisions, largely out of touch with their commands, outnumbered 5 to 1 and worse, outgunned and surprised, managed to stop the Germans in their main line of advance. The Germans never did take the Ridge.

◆   ◆   ◆

As he came over to Russ's bed the medic asked, "He still with us?"

The nurse smiled sadly. "Yes, he is, and now he's involved in some serious fighting business. He no longer talks about Fries or his brother, Wood, or even his everlasting momma. He's reliving the fighting on the 16th when his company was nearly wiped out."

Out of the Mountain Cove

"Shhh…" Hill whispered under his breath as he rejoined his fellow soldier in the brush pile. "Shhhh. Germans. Germans," he repeated in a low voice hardly loud enough to be heard even as close as the two young Americans were in their temporary hideout among the roots of a large tree.

◆　　　◆　　　◆

Earlier that evening, Russ and Charlie Hill had been summoned by Lieutenant Dominic Gaudino and given a critical assignment that mean life or death for the thirty-odd remaining members of the company trapped in the hills of Belgium.

Their unit, as a part of the 99th division, had borne the brunt of the German assault in the Ardennes forest. They were cut off, surrounded and desperate. Every time they tried to move as a unit, savage machine gun fire cut them off and they'd been forced to retreat back into a U shaped box canyon formed by three ridges.

Their backs were literally against the wall. There was little danger of an attack from the ridge behind them because of the terrain. However, every time they looked over one of the other ridges, German rifle fire kicked up snow and ice all around them.

German soldiers lay in wait at the mouth of the box canyon, which was the sort of place Russ had grown up calling a cove out in the Appalachian Mountains. Occasionally, the Krauts pretended to venture in the cove to see if the trapped Americans were alert, testing the GIs and making sure they did not rest. A few rounds always sent them back to their positions, as though they thought the GIs had more weaponry than they really did.

In larger scheme of things the Germans apparently had little to fear from this small group of forlorn soldiers. Or so it appeared at the time.

Wave after wave of Panzers had flowed through the American lines, making a beeline for the other side of the Ardennes; moving toward Antwerp and the harbor. Hitler and his army planned to cut through the massed one million Allied troops and divide the (already bickering) Americans and British. If he could capture the port and in the process secure additional fuel for both tanks and planes, the little corporal-socialist-turned-dictator believed he might buy time for his scientists to complete one of his dreamed of secret weapon of mass destruction—the atomic bomb. They were not far behind the Americans.

When Germans poured through the Ardennes in strict formation shaped largely by the hill and hollow terrain, the various elements of the 99th had been hurt bad and scattered at the initial pounding. The 99th was in danger of being destroyed, and they desperately needed to regroup.

However, GIs in this small, decimated and demoralized company of farm boys, hillbillies and whiz kids were not thinking about the big picture. They were pinned down in the box canyon, or as Squirrel called it "the holler," and it was clear that the Nazis were committed to their destruction. Half of the company was already dead or seriously wounded, the captain was dead and a mortar round had shattered their communications gear.

Trapped with limited communication, lacking a sense of direction from command, without experienced leadership and with a growing sense of despair the company was shaken. In the back of every mind in that holler was one thought *is this the way it's going to end? Here in the middle of nowhere, in the cold and snow?*

They were all volunteers, and had come to kill those damn Nazis. The unexpected pounding they'd taken from the German guns, tanks and soldiers had shattered the men's confidence in their first engagement. *Would they live to fight again? Could they get any help? How?* Those were questions in every mind.

There were fewer than thirty-five soldiers remaining out of a full company of more than a hundred and more than half of those were wounded. There were no medics or life saving morphine and the wounded died as shock set in and the numbing cold penetrated their bodies. Food supplies were limited to what each GI had in his pack, and their thin World War I uniforms were cold and soaked from the snow covered leaves they huddled beneath. There were no medical supplies whatsoever and ammunition was limited. Things did not look good.

In their retreat to this spot of precarious security, the battered company had left many of their comrades on the ground behind them. No one knew how many were dead and how many died after the Germans overran their position. Few could account for a single acquaintance or buddy.

In the holler, few men had the proper tools to dig a protective hole in the ground. Worse, the frozen, rocky ground was nearly impossible to dig. The landscape was littered with brown humps hiding GIs half dug into holes amid the snow-covered forest, sheltered by tall trees.

It may have looked peaceful, but it was a forlorn and lonely place. The men were depressed and concerned.

The soldiers huddled together the first night and spent the next day checking various escape routes, tending the wounded as best they could, dodging the occasional sniper pot shot, and hoping for something or someone to come to their aid. There was no help in sight. It was miserable.

Late that afternoon, the 2nd Lieutenant, who was the highest-ranking officer left alive, called, "Gilley! You and Hill come over here!"

The three young men (the Lieutenant was twenty three and Hill and Gilley were both twenty) huddled under a small evergreen while the officer reluctantly outlined his plan. He started by asking, "You guys are from West Virginia, right?"

"Not me," Russ replied.

"You're both hillbillies, right?" Gaudino continued.

"Not West Virginia hillbillies," Russ argued.

"Where in the hell are you from Gilley?"

"Southwest Virginia, Sir." Russ retorted.

"How is the terrain out there? Is it anything like these mountains?"

Russ nodded. "Kinda like these. Lots of hollers and such."

"What about you Hill? Is this like West Virginia?"

"Well sorter," Charlie replied, "except I grew up on the Ohio River."

"The Ohio?" Lieutenant Gaudino repeated in a Bronx accent. The short man with the prematurely receding hairline exhaled, frustrated.

"God damn it, you're both hillbillies, right?"

"Yep! Yep!" the two quickly replied, wondering where this was going. Why was the Lieutenant so interested in where they were from all of a sudden? He hadn't said anything directly to either of them since they left Boston, except to give orders and refer to them as hillbillies. It was obvious that the little Yankee had no confidence in southern boys, whether they were hillbillies or farm boys.

"Well, that's good. That's good," Gaudino announced, almost to himself. "That's good," he repeated, raising his voice ever so slightly and looking at them one at a time, studying their faces, "because I have an assignment for you two if you're up to it."

"Yes sir," they agreed one after the other, for this sounded serious.

"You guys know we're trapped in here?"

"Yes, sir. That's what everybody says," Charlie responded with Russ nodding his head in agreement added. "Is it bad?"

"Well, the damn truth is we've lost communications. And with the Captain dead over there…" Gaudino glanced at a motionless hump lying on the snow-covered ground, some distance closer to where the Germans lay in wait. "With him gone, I'm in the dark. We never discussed what to do in a case like this. We never discussed a situation like this and not back in OCS either."

It was obvious that the acting Captain was unsure and anxious and rightly so, since this was his first combat mission and it was less than eight months since he graduated from officer candidate school (OCS) and joined the 99th as they left the Boston harbor. Then in the first minutes of the German assault the Captain was killed, leaving the Lieutenant in charge. Gaudino tried to project confidence and optimism to his men even though, that effort was slipping by the hour.

Russ and Charlie traded looks and Charlie thought, *Of course you didn't expect this. Everyone thought we were going to march straight into Berlin by Christmas some said.*

The Lieutenant cleared his throat. "We're trapped. But the Germans are either being careful or they think they have a world of time to take care of us. So, though we're not in great shape, we may be able to hang in here for a couple of days. That is, if they don't decide to take us on directly—and if they do, we'll take a lot of them with us, you can bet on that." He paused, and then continued. "We need to get word to the Battalion about the situation. With communications cut off...I want to know if you two hillbillies think you can sneak out of here, make your way through the woods and find the battalion command."

The two privates looked at the officer, then at each other. Russ spoke first. "Hell anything is better than being trapped here waiting to be finished off. Right Charlie?"

"Damn Right, damn rightttt..." Hill responded with a shiver in his voice, shaken by the bitter cold. "We'll do it, Lieutenant"

The Lieutenant nodded like he hadn't expected anything else. "Well here's what I think. We'll give you whatever you need. That is, if we have it. You guys will slip out of this creek bed of a hellhole as soon as it gets dark and before the moon comes up. I want you to head west and find someone who can get word to command about our situation."

"How're we supposed to know west from east?" Charlie asked.

"I'll give you my compass. Then when the moon comes up, keep it over your right shoulder the best you can and that will take you west." The Lieutenant handed over the compass and continued his encouragement the two GIs, "There are thousands of our guys back there, and the Germans will find that out soon enough. You will be able to find another unit if you can get clear of this place." He spoke with authority then paused for a moment before wishing them, "Good luck."

Just before six o'clock that evening, just as the forest grew pitch black with oncoming night, the two GIs slipped out of the holler and headed up an east fork of the mountain stream. The last thing Gaudino did was to grab hold of each man's right forearm and look him in the eye saying, "We're depending on you guys."

"We'll do it Lieutenant," Russ responded with confidence and Charlie nodded.

"Make that Dom," was the Lieutenant's half-joking reply.

The hillbillies carried packs with ammunition—and some food. Both had pistols, while Russ had an M1 rifle. They hardly looked human as they crawled up the little steam bed and peeked over the ridge. They could have been big brown turtles. They could see nothing, not even the moon, which was due to come up soon. Maybe that was better, Russ thought as they slipped over the small knoll and down into another stream bed that his compass indicated would lead them west and hopefully closer to help.

They were off on an incredibly dangerous mission, but it was perhaps better than being pinned down in that holler. Anything seemed better than that. And besides, the two young hillbillies felt quite comfortable in the woods on their own. The Lieutenant had been right about that.

They scooted down the dry streambed feet first, moving a few feet then stopping to listen and get their bearings again. They were in a hurry, yes; however, they were equally wary of stumbling into something or someone…

In short order, they worked their way to the end of the small streambed to another larger holler, where they stopped and huddled together for several minutes. The tension was almost unbearable and while the two GIs wanted to hurry, they were careful to stop every several steps or yards to listen lest they run up on some German patrols or maybe just an individual soldier using the forest to take a leak or a crap.

Clearly the best thing for them to do was avoid confrontation under any circumstance…if they could.

To rest and get the lay of the land they hunkered down against the side of an embankment, close to the stump of a large tree that lay broken across the little holler. Russ figured his long, dark shape looked like a fallen log or a large root from the stump of the tree. Charlie looked more like a sack of chop or corn, a brown round bundle. They surveyed the scene. There was little to see in the damp, dark forest.

Suddenly, they picked up the sound of voices from just around the entrance to their streambed, over in the larger holler. It sounded like German voices. Hearts pounding, Russ and Charlie eased around the embankment and reconnoitered. They saw three of the enemy sitting around a small fire with rifles slung over their backs. One was eating something as the three talked in low, urgent tones.

Russ and Charlie exchanged looks, but before they could calculate their situation, several rifle shots and short bursts of machine gun fire shattered the night calm from a short distance away. The Germans jumped to their feet and looked up the hill, past where Russ and Charlie had just been. They swung their rifles into firing positions and began moving carefully up the hill toward the sounds of fighting.

The young hillbillies saw this as their chance and scrambled over to the campfire to look for anything that might help them. They found very little.

Disappointed, they moved further down the second, larger streambed, which still led them west. It had been more than two hours since they left their beleaguered comrades, and they had covered barely a mile. Their uniforms were soaked from the freezing mist and the snow on the leaf-covered earth. They needed to move cautiously.

They soon reached another sharp bend in the streambed, slowed down and peeked around the corner. Ahead in a large holler, a lone German soldier squatted listening for the sound of gunfire. He huddled close to the fire and there was no way they could pass undetected. So they retreated a few feet into the partial shelter of some bushes growing out and over the roots of a large tree.

"What do you think, Russ," whispered the soaked, chilled Charlie.

"Damned if I know," Russ whispered back. "Hell, your nickname is Squirrel why don't you climb that tree and jump on him?" That didn't seem like a half bad idea to Charlie, who crept out into the middle of the smaller streambed and surveyed the situation. Then he slipped back to the safety of the tree stump and blew on his hands to warm them while he thought.

After a moment, he whispered, "Russ, if I draw him up here, could you knife him?"

"Knife him?"

"Yeah, just slit his throat."

"Hmm. Damn it, Squirrel, that's bad." While Russ had seen deer, hogs and other animals get their throats slit; killing men so easily and in that manner unnerved him. He had shot several Germans over the past few days, but to slit their throats…that made him uncomfortable at best. Nevertheless, he was determined to do it if necessary to bring help to the guys back in that cove.

Charlie cocked his head. "Yep, I think we can do it. But if those other guys come back here and find us, then it'll be worse than bad."

"That's right. That sure is. We have to figure out something." Russ replied but then was silent a moment. "How would we do it?"

"Well, I could move out there in the middle of the holler and pretend I'm hurt, and when he comes up, you jump out and finish him off. We can't let him make a noise or those other Germans will head back here and finish us off." Charlie suggested.

"What if he just finishes you off first?" Russ wanted to know.

"Nah, he won't do that 'cause he wants us alive. If they didn't want us alive, the whole company up in that holler would likely have been attacked long ago."

"Hmmm…guess you might be right," Russ whispered, guts chilling at the thought. "How are we going to do it?"

"I'll just stagger out there and fall down. Then he'll come running."

"Don't you guess he might call for help?"

"Nah, then he'd look bad, and besides, it would be a real big deal for him to do something like this by himself. It might get him some extra rations or maybe more."

"If it don't, then you're fucked and my ass is up the creek without a paddle with you. You want to take that chance?"

The ever-analytical Charlie Hill replied, "Our asses are up the creek without a paddle anyway if we don't make something happen. Right? We got to get on with it."

Russ snorted ruefully. "God damn it, you're right again. Let's do it!"

Without further discussion, Hill stood up and staggered down the small holler into the larger streambed with his head down as he held his lower body and groaned, "Help, help, help me."

The young German soldier popped up, grabbed his bayoneted rifle and stared at the apparently wounded GI.

"Vas ist das?" he demanded, wondering what the other man was doing there. Too young and inexperienced to be sure of himself, he repeated to himself, *what is this? What is this?*

Charlie dropped to his knees, holding his abdomen and doing his best to lure the cautious enemy into the trap.

"Vas ist das?" the young German repeated, and then closed in to capture the wounded GI. Russ could almost see him think, *what would my buddies say if I single-handedly captured an enemy soldier? What would my captain say?*

Then Russ took a breath and leaped. He bowled the German over. Entangled, the two rolled over and over in the snow until they stopped against a small hillside. Charlie jumped up, looking for a chance to help subdue the German before he could sound an alarm.

The men struggled, Russ trying to gain control and the German struggling to retain his rifle. Just as Charlie reached them, the German boy managed to get his rifle up enough to aim from his waist and get a shot off.

The bullet hit the young West Virginian squarely in the chest, stopping him in place. The boy from Wayne County sank to the ground obviously in real trouble.

And this time he wasn't acting. He was down and in trouble.

Shock hit Russ first, and then temper and hatred for all Germans boiled over, especially for the one he was struggling with.

Shooting Charlie had distracted the young Kraut, and before he returned his attention to fighting, the huge GI was on top of him. Russ got the opening he needed, and without a second thought stabbed the Kraut in the chest, just under the ribs on the guy's left side.

Out of the corner of his eye, Russ saw Charlie squirming in the snow, bleeding fiercely. The sight infuriated Russ and he stuck the knife in the German's neck with a powerful stroke, pushing the six inch blade into the German's throat and up into his brain, then twisting it for good measure.

The German gurgled blood, his eyes rolled back and he went limp.

Russ turned his back on his dead enemy and dropped down beside Charlie, who was twitching and groaning, dying of a direct hit to the heart. It was clear that there was no saving him and for certain they had heard the shot. Time was short.

Russ couldn't believe it. His friend from the same part of the world, the guy who asked so many irritating questions, but wasn't half bad at all—he was down. Russ was devastated, shocked beyond belief. His friend from the mountains of home was dying but he had to move and in a hurry if he was to escape.

Charlie was still alive. *What can I do now Mom?* He thought what *could I do? He couldn't just jump and run. Not with Charlie dying right there.*

He pulled Squirrel into his arms. The wounded soldier spat bloody foam and whispered, "Russ?"

"Yes, Charlie," Russ responded, leaning over the West Virginian. "What is it, Charlie?"

"I want to go home."

"Home where is that?"

"Home to Ceredo," the dying man gurgled.

"Ceredo?"

"Ceredo, West Virginia," he whispered in his last breath. He slumped in a limp pile on a snow-covered hillside in a cold, damp forest that was the middle of nowhere for Charlie and all West Virginians who had ever lived.

Stunned and shaken beyond anything he had ever experienced, Russ promised, "I'll make sure you get home, Charlie. You damned hillbillies need to be in West Virginia, not here in nowhere."

As his friend slipped away, an awful feeling came over Russ. He felt as though the world had ended. In a way, a part of his world *had* ended, because he had come to depend on the confident, smart, articulate young man from the hills and valleys of the Ohio River basin. Now Squirrel was gone. A part of Russ's world had slipped away. He sat stunned and depressed, not knowing what to do now that the comrade he had come to know so well was gone.

What should I do now? Was it worth Charlie's life? Oh, Mom what can I do, what can I do? He thought.

Then he heard the sounds coming his way, someone was yelling in some god-awful language. Was it German or someone else? He wondered but he knew. Then sorrow turned to anger with the men out there, with the war. These damned Europeans and their war, their madness of fighting each other. How had the Americans ended up here, anyway? Why? Why had Squirrel had to leave his peaceful Ohio Valley home in the first place?

This was nothing like what they taught in basic. There was little glory in fighting and killing, and no one had mentioned that he would make friends only to lose them.

Then, as Russ despaired and thought about giving up, giving in a large figure appeared beside him. It wasn't a German. No, this figure spoke English and poked at him to get up and complete his mission.

Holy hell! Russ realized with a rush of surprise, *it was 'ol Jughead.* He had slipped away from their unit and followed the two hillbillies.

Frank lopped up in his gangly way grimacing now that he had caught up to his two friends but it was too late for one.

With the company decimated and dug in all around the holler, Frank had ended up at the far upper end of the cove and away from Lieutenant Gaudino. After watching Russ and Charlie leave he was anxious for action. So with everybody's attention on the Germans at the mouth of the natural mountain cove, Frank decided to ease through the woods to see exactly what the two GIs were up to slipping through the woods in the grayish misty dark.

After gaining sight of them, he followed slowly and surely without thinking that he might be getting into trouble or causing trouble for them. He had avoided any situation that might attract the attention of the any Germans that might be around in the woods and hills. However, he had arrived, too, late. They now realized they had to leave their West Virginia friend and get out of there or meet Charlie's fate.

"Russ." Frank shook Russ's shoulder and whispered, "Russ, Charlie's gone. We've got to get going. We need to get out of here and get to the battalion. We need to help our guys in the company. We've been gone for six hours now and we need to get going. Now!"

Russ shook his head as despair and anger at the Germans overtook him. "Damn those Krauts. I'm going to kill all those bastards!"

"No! Not now," Frank cautioned. "We need to get help and save the men trapped back there in the holler. Come on Russ, those Krauts are coming. We need to get out of here, or we'll be like Charlie. We need to get going now!"

Together, the young men stumbled down through the forest unaware of where they were going. They just trusted the compass that Russ had kept tied to his belt.

They kept going west, realizing that their footprints in the snow formed a trail through the Ardennes forest. They could only hope to reach the battalion before their trail was discovered leading away from the dead German soldier.

Frank grabbed his comrade's arm and the young soldiers pushed on as fast as they dared go. They stopped now and then to listen then move on, hoping to reach the American command in time to help their trapped comrades. On one of their short rest breaks, they slipped into a partially hidden spot behind a tree stump. Just in time.

Nearby, loud German voices suddenly rose. "Siehe hier im Schnee!"

"They've seen our tracks," Frank whispered. They were anxious and frozen in place as the German continued toward their position.

Then a second voice replied, "Zwei Amerikaner." There were two of them.

The two boys listened and they thought *what do we do now? Run? Lay low? What?*

"Wo sind sie?"

"Soh sehe thie spuren?"

Frank whispered to Russ, "They're following our trail in the snow."

That settled it. There was no point in hoping the German squad would miss them. The Krauts were obviously hot on their trail, running hard with the rage over their fallen comrade a fifteen-year-old boy probably on his first mission.

Not unlike the soldiers of the 99th.

Frank knew they needed to get out of there, and fast. He glanced at the Lieutenant's compass, and then motioned to Russ. They headed out at a fast walk, trying to look in every direction at once.

Luck was with them. The Germans advanced cautiously, perhaps influenced by their comrade's demise, and their slow pace allowed Russ and Frank to put some space between the two groups and quickly.

Once it seemed they were well ahead of the Germans, they stopped to think about what direction they should go. With that in mind, they stumbled around a bend in the large, meandering streamed and were shocked to see three uniformed figures. Russ immediately thought *we found them!* After a second look he whispered, *Germans!*

Reflexes now sharpened by experience, Russ and Frank fired off a couple of quick rounds and ran for cover behind the trees.

One German went down, but still got off a few shots. The others spread and began shooting with their rifles, squatting on one knee to squeeze off shots as they attempted to pick off the hidden Americans.

And just like that, Russ and Frank were hunkered down together, cut off from their command with nowhere to go.

Minutes later, it grew worse. Voices called from the hills behind them. "Wo sind sie?"

From their front they heard, "Zwei Amerikaners" and knew that they had been seen.

They were trapped; this was it.

"Well I'm not giving in," Russ whispered to Frank, who was hiding behind a tree a few feet away. It was a fight to the finish and the two young Americans were ready. There was no choice in their minds. They had heard that the Germans had no capacity for handling prisoners and that left them with no choice. They could not give up.

For what seemed an eternity, the two Americans were pinned down by occasional rifle fire as the dozen odd young Germans pondered what they would do.

Then, out of nowhere submachine gun fire sounded, heavy and deep. They ducked, thinking this was the final assault. They were done for.

Then they realized something important.

Something wonderful had happened

Americans had come!

Within minutes, a dozen or more GIs carrying rifles and submachine guns and firing at anything that moved overran the area. The Krauts had already skedaddled, leaving the Americans to rejoice in their rescue.

Russ and Frank were overcome with emotion. It was unusual for the two boy-men to be shaken, but this was different.

Their joy was short lived as their thoughts then turned back to the men trapped in the holler. The men in the cove were the crisis now. They were safe but their company was still trapped.

After a few minutes of celebration and briefing the officer in command of the company on another mission but at the right place and right time for Frank and Russ, Captain Aubrey Hilliard, mapped out a rescue plan for the eighteen or so men who would carry out the mission.

They had not encountered any additional Germans, for they had moved on heading to the sea. Within days, however, the Germans would turn and attempt to consolidate their gains by taking and securing Elsenborn Ridge, where a decimated element of the 99th was still deployed. However, for now all was quiet, a fact Hilliard intended to use.

He looked at a crumpled map, talked on the phone and drew a plan in frozen sand of the streambed. He appeared to know exactly where the company was trapped and what he wanted to do about it. The 26-year-old Captain (field-commissioned like Gaudino) was determined to pull off the rescue, and if he had doubt, the GIs never guessed it.

After their briefing, the men quickly gathered themselves and began moving back to the holler, following the snow trail that had almost proved Russ and Frank's undoing. They hurried, stomping the single-file trail as they ran to the rescue. Captain Hilliard spread the combined force with scouts on both flanks. No one thought of the fleeing Germans, for the Hilliard group had the superiority in numbers and experience.

As they passed Charlie, still, partially snow-covered, several soldiers doffed their hats, realizing that it could just as easily have been them. Russ paused, and then ran; the best way for him to honor Charlie was to see their mission accomplished.

Within an hour the force approached the holler. They saw that
Gaudino's company had propped up some bodies of dead GIs in partially concealed position to give a false impression of strength and
numbers.

Captain Hilliard quietly motioned a halt, then summoned Russ and
Frank plus a couple of noncommissioned officers to crouch down
around him on the forest floor. The officer using the forest floor drew a
map of the terrain and the approximate location of the trapped company, then asked Russ and Frank to confirm the map and give their
opinions. While Russ was unusually withdrawn, Frank was full of
ideas. He wanted to take on the Germans head on pinning them
between his company in the hills and the fresh advancing force.

Hilliard decided that six of the men would take ammunition and
some supplies and follow Russ and Frank back to their pinned-down
comrades. The Captain would lead the remainder of the force to encir-
cle the entrenched Germans from a distance and move rapidly once
those in the holler were armed and ready together they would create
crossfire.

As Frank and Russ led the group slowly back in the cove toward
their pinned down company, Russ quietly whistled Dixie, hoping the
Bronx-born Lieutenant would recognize the tune they had teased him
with on the ship coming over from Boston. Sure enough, the muddy,
weary Lieutenant slipped out to meet them in the early dawn. The hillbillies had been gone for more than six hours, and Lieutenant Gaudino
was overwhelmed to see the rescue party and two of his boys, Russ and
Frank.

Tears flowed down Gaudino's dirty, bloody face as he greeted the
men. To see them and the help they brought was more than he ever
had dreamed of when he sent them out just hours before.

As soon as the greetings and celebrations were over, Gaudino looked
intently at the AWOL Frank and pretended to be upset, "God Damn
it, Mitchell! What the hell have you been doing? We needed you here.
Your ass is in real trouble!!"

Russ stepped up and reported, "God, Lieutenant, I couldn't have done it without him. Frank made it possible."

Gaudino half grinned and responded with his eyes moist, "If this damn thing ever ends and I go home, I'm moving down to West Virginia with you guys." The three comrades stood together arms extended and hands on each other's shoulders savoring the moment.

Later as morning approached the men up the holler whispered to each other excitedly but quietly as meager supplies and ammunition were distributed. All were aware of the rescuers and the combined action, which awaited the break of dawn. Then as the light spread gently across the forest floor all their attention was focused on the mouth of the cove and the disturbed forest in between. They waited on the Captain for the signal to attack. Once it came more than two-dozen GIs had arms ready and focused on the enemy lines. Their chance was coming.

With a howl, the rescuers opened fire on the unsuspecting Germans at the crack of dawn, killing several immediately. The ragtag company in the holler joined the fight with everything they had, including machine guns and rifles, creating a withering crossfire that no enemy could withstand for long. There was no quarter. Many Germans were gunned down, as they appeared to want to surrender. American boys barely out of high school became angry killing machines. There would be no quarter.

And so the company was liberated and the men were saved. However, the celebration was short lived…especially for Russ.

Damn Right it Hurts

Only a few hours earlier, everything had been so different.

"Brrrrrrr...." Russ muttered almost under his breath as he beat his arms and shoulders with gloved hands in an effort to keep the circulation going. He glanced at Frank Mitchell, the tall skinny guy from Indiana. "Damn this cold. Why can't the Army get us some warm clothes?"

In the winter of 1944, the massive army Eisenhower had convened on the German border was so short of supplies that many American soldiers in Western Europe were clothed in World War I uniforms—the best the U. S. could do at the time; a fact that wasn't well known then and didn't get much attention later. All that most people remember is how we won the war.

The two young Americans, not yet old enough to vote, were spending Christmas Eve 1944 together in an icy, muddy foxhole on Elsenborn Ridge in Belgium. Their constant companions, other than the paper back novel in Jughead's pocket, was a 50 caliber machine gun propped on a little dirt knoll they had fashioned on the east side of their 'hole, and the intermittent flashes of light from artillery firing in the freezing, misty, foggy distance.

The landscape was eerie. Just a few days earlier, beautiful evergreen trees had grown on the Belgian ridge. Now it was a wreck of a forest with splintered trees everywhere and mud mounds where GIs had dug foxholes in the frozen ground to provide some protection from the enemy. The men had fashioned makeshift roofs for their foxholes by lacing shell-broken tree limbs over the holes, and then gathering pine boughs knocked off by mortar and artillery fire and used them to both camouflage the foxhole and provide some shelter from the falling snow.

The gentle flakes drifting down to the earth made the boys think of Christmas back home. The flickering campfires in the distance only added to their longing.

Inside the 'holes, pairs and trios of young American soldiers, most still waiting for their 21ˢᵗ birthdays, sat shivering under blankets as they reminisced of times spent together since joining the U.S. Army. Last Christmas Eve, most of them had been in the States and many had been on furlough with family and friends. Just a month earlier, they had been encamped on the German Border in the Ardennes Forest, holding an uncontested line. That's why Ike had placed the inexperienced 99ᵗʰ Division at this particular point along the front—the Germans weren't expected to attack it. Why would they? It was a difficult stretch of terrain that held no particular strategic importance. The Belgians knew different, for it was a time-honored fact that the Germans always advanced on their neighbor through that stretch of the Ardennes. The Allied brass apparently ignored those rumors if it ever got all the way up the ladder, just as the talk among the villagers about increased activity that winter just across the border in Germany was not taken that serious.

The young soldiers had all enjoyed the recent Thanksgiving holiday, even though their accommodations had been half tents and more-or-less secure, hand-built bunkers. Their dinners had been warm, though the weather was bitter cold and their uniforms weren't heavy enough to shut out the cold air or the ever-present moisture. Glances across the river had shown them Germans trudging about in long trench coats, which surely were much warmer than the U.S. uniforms. Rather than the weather talk had turned to hopes of pushing on to Berlin and ending this dirty war with Germany. Perhaps, the soldiers had mused over turkey and the whistling wind, this would happen in January or March, at the latest. *Then can we go home?* That was the thought dominating their minds. *Home. Oh, only to go home.* People back in the

U.S. missed their young soldiers, but nothing like the boys missed home and Christmas and friends, and most of all family.

Yes, Thanksgiving had been quiet—but soon thereafter things changed.

> *Once the Germans poured across the temporary border, or front, on the 16th of December, 1944, creating the largest and deadliest battle of the war, everyone—from whiz kid to farm boy, from hillbilly to cook, from mechanic to medic—became a fighting man; soldiers on the front line ruthlessly killing and struggling to survive in a battle that saw 80,000 American casualties in thirty days as well as another 160,000 Germans wounded and killed. In the midst of battle, cooking became less a community project and more an individual effort of chewing prepackaged K-Rations. On that day, in December of 1944, the 99th Infantry Division had been surprised and overwhelmed by German soldiers pouring across the border. In a disorganized, disorienting rag tag retreat, the 99th had pulled back to form a line, digging in on the largely uncontested Elsenborn Ridge as the Germans swarmed past, following the natural terrain to penetrate deep and fast through American lines. The Krauts were on a mission to divide the Allies and capture the seaport. Because of this, even though the 99th had suffered dramatically in the first hours, they were able to dig in and go toe to toe when the enemy turned back to destroy them.*

On Christmas Eve, eight days after they'd first dug into the ridge, Russ and Frank settled into their 'hole and watched the night sky light up not too far away. Russ, the big overgrown hillbilly from the town of Fries in the Blue Ridge Mountains of Virginia, fitted right in with the rest of this Division. The 99th as was well know by then was made up of self-described hillbillies, farm boys and 'whiz' kids—the latter being young college students who had enlisted full of dreams of becoming Army administrators, pilots and officers—until they were sent to the front where they were more desperately needed. On this particular cold and dreary December day, Russ and his friends were just a few of the thousands of green GIs whose hours and days were numbered.

Back in Boston as they readied to board ships bound for England and even later they came to think of Russ Gilley as a big, happy go lucky guy out for a good time. However, like so many other boyish GIs, when the time arrived he became a man on the spot and did what he had come to Europe for—to stand up and fight the damned Germans. They promised it was to save America, to save civilization, though most of those boys would have had difficulty spelling, much less defining "civilization."

They did what they needed to. Starting the first day after the Germans overran their position. After that day, Russ was never again a cook, though his friends still teased him. They knew him for what he had done, not what he would yet do in the time remaining to him.

"Damn it Cookie, why in the hell can't you cooks do better than this?" Frank groused, munching on a stale piece of bread, his head covered by a blanket taken from a dead German. "In Indiana we never stooped to eating this, not even during the Depression."

"Hell, I've been having too much fun burning Germans for the last two weeks to worry about cooking," replied Russ. He didn't bother mentioning that he was dreaming about his mother's canned pork tenderloin and warm biscuits. He had told his Mom that he wanted to fight the Germans. Even though he wasn't old enough to enlist, she had reluctantly given in and signed the necessary papers. Well, he had finally gotten his chance to fight when the Germans launched their 600,000 troops and tanks through the Ardennes, but it hadn't exactly been the glorious combat the recruiter had described.

War was bloody. It was cold. And it was downright scary.

Because of that, it helped to think of home. He'd even adopted a phrase from his youth in the cotton mill town of Fries. Back then, 'burning' meant making someone pay for his misdeed or mistakes. Now, he was burning Germans.

"Hey Russ, I hear ol' Patton is pawing the ground wanting to come and rescue us," Frank yelled over the constant howl of incoming mortar fire. He was always analyzing things.

"Hell, I heard the Captain say they need him over at Bastogne worse than we need him here. Besides, this mud would mess up his spit-polished boots." Russ glanced at his friend's blanket-wrapped form and thought, it's *about time we changed places for a while.* But he didn't say it out loud because he and Mitchell had been through a "whole bunch" together. Instead, he asked, "Course, some help wouldn't be so bad right now, would it? Yeah, that Patton he sure won't shy away from a fight, that's for sure. He's won his share of medals."

At the mention of medals, the farm boy's head emerged from its blanket cocoon. The blanket fell from his shoulders and he said, "Russ, I heard the rumor that you might get a medal yourself. What in the hell?" Frank whistled approvingly, a sound that was mimicked by the shells flying above them.

When he didn't get an answer, he repeated, "What the hell?" just in case Russ hadn't heard him the first time.

"Hell, Jughead You were there and you did more," Russ answered as he amused himself by aiming his 50-caliber gun, first on an imagined German outpost, then on what might have been a soldier walking through the forest. "What does the brass care about the average Joe out here, anyway? Stars, what the hell." Russ muttered a curse under his breath. He thought, *now that the game is down to scratch, nobody cares about that shit.*

Now and again, a German flare exploded along the distant skyline, lighting the horizon. With the help of those red flashes, Russ could see down the crosshairs of his gun as he aimed it at imaginary targets and tried not to think how it felt to actually kill a man.

"Why can't you shoot another deer so we can cook it over a fire like we did the week after Thanksgiving?" Frank asked, needling Russ a little bit. They might be in the middle of a fight to the death but the spirit of the young American warriors was still intact.

"Ain't been no deer in these parts since the Krauts begin firing their 88's. The deer used their brains and high-tailed it out of here long ago.

They left us dumb GIs and loggerheaded Krauts to fight over this God damned chunk of mud, ice and snow."

"Where'd you learn to shoot deer like that, anyhow?" Mitchell asked, searching for conversation that would help take their minds off the distant whistling shells and the damp cold.

"Damn it, Frank," Russ replied, annoyed enough to use the Hoosier's given name, "growing up in the hills of southwest Virginia weren't like the corn fields of Indiana. If you didn't hunt, there weren't much meat on the table. Mom sent me out with my brother Wood when I was just ten-years-old. When I was twelve she sent me hunting by myself. We killed deer, groundhogs, 'coons, rabbits, squirrels and most anything else that walked, and we ate most of our kill."

"You ate groundhogs?"

Russ didn't bother to answer, and the 'hole fell silent as the young soldiers drifted back to their boyhoods and thought about the good times they had left behind to join the army and fight in Europe.

"Indiana's got pheasants and quail," Frank reminisced with a satisfied smile, not at all concerned by his friend's irritation.

"Yeah, I heard of that. Wood was always talking about quail, pheasants and grouse—he loved to hunt birds." Russ glanced back at his 'hole mate. "You guys had all those corn fields and lots more birds for hunting than us. Wood always wanted to go to Indiana to hunt pheasants. Hell, he traded a seventeen-jeweled watch that his wife Forest bought him on their first wedding anniversary for a sixteen-gage shotgun and a birddog pup. It made her mad as hell. Mom didn't think it was a smart way to spend money either, and she said so," Russ rambled on, annoyance giving way to shivers as the cold set deeper into his bones.

"Hey? Hey!" A voice startled them, sounding clear as a bell in the night air.

Russ peeked out over the lip of their 'hole to see who was yelling. It was ol' Mike, better known as "Rabbit", McAllister. The guy from the mountains of North Carolina was jumping and waving hands, seemingly oblivious to the Germans as he worked to get the attention of the two GIs in the adjacent foxhole.

"Hey guys? Hey, Russ? Hey, Jug? That you guys over there?"

"Yeah, it's us," Russ replied. As Frank pulled the blanket back and eased up to look north at the neighboring foxhole, Russ continued, "What do you want? Better keep your damn head down or they'll blow it off."

"Hey! Hey!" McAllister yelled all the while scrambling across the mud field that separated their holes and blurted out, "Do you guys have any chewing tobacco?" Without waiting for an invite, he jumped in their 'hole, which was barely large enough for two people.

"Nah, we don't have any chewing tobacco. Where do you think we're from, Nort' Carolina?" Russ didn't figure he needed to let on that all of his folks had come from Asheville, North Carolina and that his daddy had done some tobacco farming.

"Man we are freezing over there. Don't be such an asshole." McAllister retorted as he pulled his helmet off to reveal short, already thinning light brown hair. He nudged Russ. "I said, 'y'all got any chaw? Or maybe cigarettes?'"

Russ considered it. "Well, that's another question. Jug, do we got any cigarettes?"

Mitchell snuggled down further under his blanket and pretended not to hear. Cigarettes were scarce and McAllister was a chain smoker. Frank thought, *hell, let the damned hillbilly get his own.*

"Jug?" Russ asked in an irritated tone.

Frank relented. "Yeah, I got a couple. Take these, Mike," he said, using Rabbit's real name. Dropping the nickname signaled a certain level of seriousness. *The guy needed a cigarette for his nerves, for God's sake.*

The three GIs snuggled in the blanket deep in the foxhole, puffing cigarettes. The fog and mist lifted to reveal an awesome landscape torn up like a hurricane had come through, but the wet penetrating cold didn't change. It still cut through their thin wool uniforms. It wasn't like home or even an Army tent. But it was better than the bitter fighting they'd been living with for more than a week. It looked like maybe, just maybe the bulk of the German army had gone past the 99th and left them isolated there on the ridge pinned down by occasional frequent artillery fire. That was sure okay by them for now. Who the hell wanted to look for a fight? They'd already had their share.

What they didn't know was that the German high command had decided that Elsenborn Ridge had to be taken. The central fight in the Battle of the Bulge was about to begin.

At dawn a full-scale assault began, just as the three friends hunkered down in their foxhole to puff on stale cigarettes.

Pow! Pow! Pow! The dirt and mud flew as German machine guns sprayed bullets across the line of foxholes.

The sky opened up with 88's and mortars raining down on the American positions. All of the soldiers ducked into their foxholes. All of them, that is, except Rabbit. He knew that Johnnie, another one of those West Virginia hillbillies, needed him to help feed their 50-caliber, especially if the Germans planned on coming up the ridge once the American line was softened.

Called by duty, he jumped out of the safe 'hole and dashed across the muddy, torn up earth heading for his own gun buddy.

Russ yelled to no avail, "Mike! Mike! No! No! Come back!"

McAllister ran as fast as he could across the torn earth, dodging from one mound to another in a zigzag pattern, for a moment looking just like the Rabbit for which he was named.

An enormous amount of machine gun fire spewed down. Rabbit was hit in one shoulder, then in both legs. He went down in the mud and frozen slush halfway to his 'hole. He fell in a cross-legged position, both legs useless, and moaned, clutching his lower chest where several rounds had found their mark.

From his foxhole, Russ heard a pause in the shelling. The whole ridge-top was engulfed in a frightening silence, with the sole exception of McAllister's moans. The wounded boy's begging was clear to those in the nearest foxholes and caught the attention of the enemy, who occasionally fired a round at the boy.

Russ threw a leg over the lip of his 'hole, intending to help Mike, only to be tackled by Frank and pulled back.

"Damn, somebody's got to go help him," Russ hollered, trying to free himself.

"God damn it Russ, don't you go and get yourself killed!" Frank pleaded wrapping his arms and legs around the much larger Russ to pull him back into their foxhole and out of danger.

Mike's cries and moans were crystal clear, unnerving all the GIs within hearing distance.

Then, Russ tore free from Frank, rolled out of their foxhole and headed for Mike, running in a zigzag pattern just as they had been taught. The Germans caught sight of him and opened fire, spraying bullets all along the ridge, kicking up dirt all around Russ.

He slithered in the mud as though he was sliding into third base during a Sunday baseball game back home in Eagle Bottom. "Hang on Mike; I'll get you out of here." This appeared doubtful. Mike had lost the use of both legs and blood was pouring from his left side, dampening his uniform to a dark black in the early morning light. "We have to get you out of here boy. You need a medic." Russ yanked Mike's coat and shirt open to get a better look at the wound.

In the background, Russ could hear Frank yelling with all the power in his large frame, "Medic!" Over here! We need a medic! Mike's down! We need a medic. We need him now, Mike's down!"

Suddenly there was a pause in the machine gun fire. All the Germans had ceased firing as if on command. The two men lay flat in the mud. The lack of noise was eerie. Realizing that something had to be done, Russ hollered, "Jug, we gotta get outta here. Rabbit's bleeding bad. He needs help; he needs a shot of the stuff."

Frank's voice rang out across the hillside "Stay there! Russ, you stay right there. I've called the medics. They'll get you guys. Just wait!"

"Damn it, I told you he's bleeding bad. We need to do something now. I'm bringing him over there. Damn the dirty Krauts…"

"Stay down, stay down!" was the answer even as Russ struggled to his knees, squirming in the mud to gain enough leverage to sling Mike over his shoulder.

With a quick jerk, ox-strong Russ Gilley stood up, and as if throwing a sack of chop over his shoulder, lifted the wounded GI and began the hundred-foot walk back to the foxhole. With the mud and the dead weight of Mike on his shoulder, Russ was slower and his zigzagging was not as quick and precise. In fact, he moved so plodding that it was like slow motion. The whole world seemed to slow down as the two crept to safer ground.

Even as the machine guns began again to spray bullets all around the two men, everything seemed to be frozen in time for those watching the two GIs making their way across the field. Finally, Russ reached the foxhole where Frank watched and waited. Machine gun bullets kicked up dirt in their path and all around the 'hole. The Krauts' mortars had resumed their pounding of the ridge top position, and the landing rounds kicked up muddy geysers destroying the few sad trees that remained.

Miraculously, there were no direct hits on the American positions.

When he reached the 'hole, Russ hefted Mike in his arms like a baby, and jumped into the 'hole feet first. Frank helped as best he could, using a blanket to cover his comrade. Russ exhaled with relief was grateful to be clear of the line of fire, back in the 'hole. The wonderful, secure foxhole or dugout felt like home.

The two soldiers tried to make the seriously wounded Mike more comfortable all the while yelling at the tops of their voices for a medic.

The incoming enemy fire had intensified. Mortar shells landed closer and everywhere, creating a deafening roar but there was no panic among the American GIs on the front line. Then they became fighting men.

The two medics already moving up the hill scampered over to the hole where Frank, Russ and Mike waited. At the ominous scream of incoming artillery fire, the rescue team hit the muddy ground and everyone looked for cover.

A shell detonated in the foxhole straight ahead—the one they were trying to reach.

Timbers flew. Mud splattered the landscape, hitting the crouching medics and others who ran to the rescue. Everything was turned upside down.

Unhurt and re-energized, the medics scrambled the rest of the way to the 'hole. There, they saw a devastating mess.

Just before the shell hit, Russ threw his body over Mike and, in the process, he'd also shielded Frank.

Nothing had shielded Russ.

Through the blood, dirt and icy mud, the medics saw two, perhaps three wounded GIs. Quickly, the lead medic grabbed Russ and turned him over. His right leg was torn into pieces and a mass of blood gushed from his right side. It was obvious that the wounds were serious. The medic jerked out a vial of morphine and gave the large soldier a double dose in his right shoulder, which seemed like the only part of the boy GI's body that wasn't damaged.

The medic motioned for the two men with the sled to remove Russ and take him down the hill to the safety of the forward aid station, which was already overcrowded. Then he turned his attention to the other two soldiers—Mike McAllister and Frank Mitchell. It was evident that Mike, too, was seriously injured. He received the next shot of morphine along with makeshift bandages to cover his wounds and stabilize him long enough to wait for a second sled.

Mitchell had been sheltered from the main force of the exploding shell. He was slightly wounded, but shook off offers of help and moved to assist with Mike as the medics and a rifleman carried Russ down the hill on a sled.

As they approached the aid station "Whiz Kid" Carson came running up to see who or what was on the sled. The recent college student saw hillbilly Russell Gilley. He grabbed the sled to help and while carrying his comrade asked, "Does it hurt, Russ? Does it hurt?"

The not unexpected answer from the ever-frank Russ, clutching his bloody side was, "Damn right it hurts, Whiz."

Earning Her Gold Star

Waiting and Then Waiting Some More

The dark green automobile stopped in the gravel driveway and two army officers got out, straightened their brown uniforms and tugged at their caps before they started up the walk to the front of the house. Oda peered out at them through the windowpane.

Knowing the purpose of the officers' visit without being told, she sank to the floor and began crying. "Oh my God, my God, it's Russ. It's my baby, my baby boy. Russ, I told you but you won't listen. Why did you have to go? Why? Why?"

She turned to her six-year-old grandson, the only other person in the room, and announced, "See what happens when you don't mind? See what happens?"

The little boy nodded silently. He was only six. What else could he do?

By that evening, word had spread throughout the Fries area that Russell Gilley had been wounded at a place called Elsenborn Ridge in faraway Belgium. That night family gathered at Oda's house in Eagle Bottom, drawn together in tragedy. The evening was one they would all remember for the rest of their lives. Would he live? That was the question on everyone's mind but one that nobody dared ask out loud, for Oda was distraught. Her life was torn asunder. Her favorite child, her baby boy lay wounded in some faraway field hospital in Europe

The living room, sitting room and kitchen of Oda's house all were filled with her children and grandchildren along with other relatives and some of Russ's friends. The news had spread like wildfire throughout the Fries area and the traffic on the dirt and gravel road was heavier as people drove by as a way of expressing their concern.

It was a gloomy night, a tense time and a time of puzzlement and bewilderment for the six-year-old boy, Wade Gilley, who saw his world crumbled by the announcement. He didn't understand all of it, but he grasped enough to know that Uncle Russ had been hurt in a battle in the war far away.

And nobody knew whether he would ever come home.

The next several days were cloaked with gloom. Oda paced the floor, constantly looking out the window at the driveway. Little Wade was there with her. He was subdued, worried for his Uncle Russ and confused by the way his all-powerful, all-knowing grandmother had been driven to her knees by the news.

Oda spent her days cooking and serving and eating meals while constantly watching the road, looking for that car that would, she was sure, pull into the driveway. She knew in her heart of hearts that Russ had moved on to the other world, the next realm, and the world her Cherokee ancestors had taught her to expect. Oda was more than a Cherokee; she was a Hard Shelled Primitive Baptist and believed in everlasting life and in saving grace. Was Russ saved? Could she pray him to her side at Judgment Day like the Mormons do? Those questions haunted Oda, for she had no clear answers. In the end she came back to her Cherokee roots…there would be another day. But that didn't pacify her.

Her heart was broken and her children feared that it would never be repaired. Without understanding why or how, she was entering a time that would be long and difficult.

◆   ◆   ◆

"I just knew that he didn't have a chance," the nurse commented looking down at the body now covered from toe to head in that tent hospital in Belgium. "But I kept hoping."

"We never know, we just do out best," the medic standing by her side comforted her. They had become emotionally attached to the young man who in his dreams had told them so much about his life and his family.

"I wonder what will happen to her."

"Her?"

"His mother, Oda," the nurse responded quietly as though it should have been obvious. "They were close."

"All these boys have mothers," the medic stated, turning away to the next bed. "Let's focus on the ones we can still help."

The nurse didn't leave Russ right away. She stared down at him, hoping he'd gone someplace warmer, without pain, where he'd one day be reunited with the family she'd come to know through his delirious ramblings.

Then she patted his hand one last time, tucked it beneath the soiled white sheet and pulled the cloth over his face.

◆   ◆   ◆

Some time later, as though The Creator himself had known she needed time to prepare herself for the news, another Army car pulled into the driveway and another team of officers came to the door and knocked. Oda knew even before they said a word.

Russ had died at a place called Elsenborn Ridge in the Ardennes Mountains of Belgium in the massive battle of all battles.

He was one of tens of thousands of American boys wounded as they stood up and stopped Hitler's last-ditch effort. He was one of thousands of young hillbillies, farm boys and whiz kids who, though inexperienced in battle, stood up to be counted and give their lives. Russ had gone to confront the Germans and Hitler and he had done exactly that. But he had also lost his life in the effort.

Mourning swept across Eagle Bottom, Hawkstown, Hilltown and the entire Fries area that day and lasted for months—or longer. A boy they had all known had fallen. To his friends and family it seemed just yesterday that Russ had been beside them…it had happened so fast. And was so, so certain.

All Oda knew was that her baby boy Russ was dead and it was her responsibility. She had done it. She had let him go to war, and now he lay dead in a grave in Belgium. She had known even before she answered the door. She also knew what had to happen next. She had to bring Russ home.

She wanted him back and would do whatever it took. Many American boys killed at the Bulge and other European battles would remain forever in graves marked by countless white crosses.

From the beginning, Oda was determined to bring her baby boy home.

The Gold Star

Countless American soldiers have earned Bronze and Silver Stars and other recognitions for bravery. Ever since World War I, the Gold Star has been reserved for mothers who lost sons (and daughters) in battle. To lose a brother or sister or husband or wife in battle is horrible, but the pain and anguish that mothers feel is the most searing, the most eternal. Brothers and sisters go on to live their lives, marrying, having careers and children, and so the love and the living of life blunt the pain of losing a loved one. However, a mother never recovers. No one can take the place of a lost child. It seems unnatural for a child to precede a parent in death but it is particularly difficult for mothers to have a child grabbed from their families and sent to another country to die a gruesome death in the heat of battle.

In 1921 The Gold Star Mothers of America was formed; this organization was very visible during the Second World War. These mothers suffer with pride but have also been known to question why their sons and daughters had to die while others, including those who avoided service, lived on.

Many times over the years, Gold Star Mothers have proven problematic for governmental leaders. Like the veterans they were problematic for President Hoover, as mothers who had lost sons in World War I came to Washington to confront Hoover about the neglect of veterans and their families at the height of the Great Depression. They were also problematic for Presidents Johnson and Nixon as mothers who lost children in the Vietnam War were even more distraught that their children fought and died for nothing.

And once again, Gold Star Mothers appeared in 2004 almost daily at the Dover Air Force Base in Delaware, the official mortuary for those servicemen and women who lost their lives in Iraq and other parts of the modern day "War on Terror."

I Want Him Home

Back in 1944, as one mother in particular prayed for her son's safety, she had no thought of stars, gold or otherwise. She just wanted her baby boy home safely.

"Wood, I want to bring him home," Oda announced to her eldest son as she sat on her front porch in the early spring of 1945. Her determination showed in her face.

After a long pause, her eldest son pulled on his Camel and questioned her, "Why, Mom?" He had long ago learned it was better to move on when folks died. He'd learned that in 1934, when his father had died and he was left to be the man in charge of the family. "Why do you need to bring him home?"

"Just gonna do it," she retorted.

"Momma, he's gone. Russ is gone. We'll never see him again."

She replied quietly, "Yes, but I'm not done."

Wood sighed, knowing there was no talking her out of things when she got that look on her face. "What do you want to do?"

"I want to bring him home so he can be buried here, not in some far away place," she retorted. Her voice was calm. Oda wasn't so emotional now—she was real determined.

Attempting to change the subject, Wood gazed through the small cloud of cigarette smoke, and gently responded, "I saw your Gold Star. You put it back up?"

"Yes," she replied. "Yes, I understand the meaning now."

"The meaning?" Wood shrugged as though the meaning was obvious to him. "They give those to the mothers who have lost a son in battle. It's a way of honoring a boy, of saying, *we honor Russ*."

"No, Wood, that ain't it." Oda gazed out over the hills on that summer night as she paused for the longest minute. "The lady told me that the Silver Star, the Bronze Star, the Medal of Honor, and all the others—those honor the soldier. The Gold Star honors the mother of a fallen soldier, because only the mother knows what it means. Only the mother who gave birth knows. That is why they give it to the mother and always have."

"So you'll always have it in your window for all to see?"

"Maybe, if I get my boy back then we'll see."

"What can I do, Mom?"

"Nothing now. If we get him back, then…" Though neither mentioned it they both knew that Russ's dog tags a primary means of battlefield identification had not been found.

Russ had been hit by a mortar round, which had done horrific damage to his body. Two of his fellow GIs had identified him, and he had been buried in Belgium without any real concrete identification. That was both a concern…And a sliver of hope for a depressed, tortured mother.

"I know Mom, I know, and I'll do it if I can, if I have to," Wood promised, all the time dreading the time and place that he would once again assume his responsibility as the man of his mother's family.

They sat for a while in the quiet summer night, with fireflies buzzing low to the ground and Oda's grandson dashing here and there attempting to catch some in a paper bag.

Finally Wood asked, "Mom, what are you going to do?"

"Well, Reba and me, we're writing the Army. I want some answers, no matter how long it takes to get them."

"Mom." Wood replied. "I need to say something about all of this."

"What?" she replied with some irritation for when her eldest spoke like he wanted to tell her that she was doing something that he did not approve of and she didn't need that.

"Well, all I wanted to say is that Rebe needs to be happy."

"Well, Woodrow what makes you think that she's not happy. She seems happy enough to me."

"Mom, Rebe loves you and she loves to be with you but she will need her own home sooner or later and everybody wants their own. Rebe is one of the prettiest girls in all the Fries area. The boys just goggle at her when she goes downtown or anywhere. Everybody thinks that you have her on a string." Oda's eldest continued.

"What do you mean that she needs her own? She's got a family."

"Mom, do you remember when you lived at grandpa's house? They needed and loved you and you loved them but you had a longing to go out and have your own life? You were 24 when you got married and Rebe is now 23. Remember?"

Oda shook her head as thought she didn't want to hear this but her son continued. "Rebe will always be here for you mom but you need to make a way for her to have a life, a future…. after you. Do you know what I mean?"

After a long and uncomfortable silence sitting on the front porch staring out into the darkness Oda responded, "I remember being at my grandpa's and it were no fun. This is different. Reba is my baby daughter and I need her. I so need her. She understands me."

"I know, mom, just think about it. Please?" He pleaded.

"Well Wood, I see what you are saying and it makes sense. I just don't know what to do right now."

May, 1945—The First Letter

"Mom! We got a letter from the Army today. Here, Mom! Here!" Reba waved the letter as she walked up the long set of steps to the front porch of their house. She had a smile on her face hoping against hope that it would be the information they sought.

That day, like most every other day, they sat on the front porch from dinner, the midday meal, until the rural postman came driving down Eagle Bottom Road to put their mail in the rickety old box. He always came just after three-thirty, like clockwork, but every day they began looking for him at least an hour early…just in case.

A drawn, sorrowful Oda slowly rose from her chair and met Reba at the top of the steps. She reached for the envelope, sat down and looked at it for the longest time. Tears came to her eyes and she almost whispered haltingly, "They did answer. I told you they would. I told you and Wood and Ruby and all. And they did."

"Mom, we told you they would, but that it would take time. The war was going on for so long, but now that things are about to end, they have time. We told you." Reba reached over gently touching her mother's hand. "Mom, do you want me to read it to you?"

Oda, now in her mid fifties, looked up as though awaking from a dream, eased back in her chair and agreed, "Sure go ahead and read it."

"Sure read it to me now."

Reba took the letter settled down in a straight-backed chair with a woven seat. Then she, too, stared at the unopened letter for a long time. This was the first communication they had really received since the final telegram in February confirming that Russ had died.

She carefully opened the letter and read the typed document to herself. Then she read it aloud to her mother. The following is the essence of that letter, gathered from Russ's Army Death File (DF) at the Department of the Defense.

May 19, 1945
Mrs. Oda Gilley
Fries, Virginia
Dear Mrs. Gilley
The Army Effects Bureau has received from overseas some property of
your son PFC Russell Gilley.
This Property, consisting of a few small items, is being sent you in a
more appropriate container…It should arrive within days.
Yours Very Truly,
P, L. KOOB
2ⁿᵈ. Lt. Q M. C.
Kansas City, Missouri

Items included:
MISC Insignia
Ribbons and Decoration
Bill Fold (empty)
Religious Items (Bible)

"A Bible?" Oda asked looking up, obviously shaken. Russ had not
been religious even though she had tried her best to get him to go to
church. *What was he doing with a bible?* She asked herself. *Had he come
to know Jesus after all?*

"Yes," Reba confirmed, "it says he had a bible."

"It was that bible I gave him when he went to boot camp. Bless his
heart," Oda mumbled at this startling and welcome news dabbing her
eyes with the small piece of cloth in her hand.

"Guess so," Reba whispered, also wiping tears from her eyes.

"So he had it until the end," Oda announced, mostly to herself. "He
had it to the end." That conclusion seemed to bring some measure of
satisfaction to this Hard Shelled Primitive Baptist who would never see
her baby again.

"Yes, he did," Reba assured her momma. "Yes, he did."

◆   ◆   ◆

Before that day, Oda had many written letters to the Army seeking information about her son, and she would send many, many more. She was courteous but ever persistent, as was her way...persistent, unrelenting. The following are some of her writings, taken from Russ's Army DF. Reba handwrote them all, presumably.

June 12, 1945
Dear Sir,
I am sorry to bother you but I have received the box of my son Russell Gilley's possessions. I was very grateful but I wanted to know did you find his dog tag?
Sincerely yours,
Oda O. Gilley.

There was no record of a reply to this letter. Perhaps, it was because the United States was pursuing the defeat of the Japanese in the Far East and pacifying a torn and bloody Europe. Like other mothers, Oda was obsessed with her son and getting his body home. Her letters were courteous as she continued to write, somehow understanding that persistence was important.

August 6, 1945
Dear Sir,
Please give me all the information you have about the location of the remains of my son PFC Russell Gilley.... and the possibility of his remains being shipped home after the war.
Yours very truly,
Oda O. Gilley.

Again she wrote after months of no response from the War Department.

March 3, 1946
Dear Sir,
My son was killed overseas and I would like all the information possible about the return of his remains. If you could send me any additional information I would surely appreciate it.
Sincerely,
Oda O. Gilley,

The U. S. Army was dutiful in their responses, but with so many American boys killed overseas it was not easy. More than 20,000 soldiers had been killed at The Bulge alone, making for a torrent of information. Slowly, Oda and her family learned more.

10 September 1945
Dear Mrs. Gilley,
Acknowledgement is made of your letter requesting information regarding on the place of burial and the return of the remains of your son, the late Private First Class Russell J. Gilley.
Now that Japan has been defeated, the immediate plans are being formulated with a view to returning to the next of kin the remains of their loves ones.
This office regrets, sincerely, the delay in answering your letter and wishes to extend its deepest sympathy in the loss of your son.
Sincerely yours,
ARTHUR L. WARREN
Colonel, QMC, Assistant.

17 December 1945
Dear Mrs. Gilley,

The official report of internment shows that the remains of your son were interred in the United States Military Cemetery #1, Henri Chapelle, Belgium, Plot BBB Row 10, Grave 184. With reference to other larger cities, the approximate location of Henri Chapelle is seven miles southwest of Aschen, Germany, five miles northwest of Eupen and eight miles east of Liege, in Belgium.

Sincerely yours,
Arthur L. Warren
Colonel QMC, Assistant

As she finished reading this letter, a red-eyed Reba looked at her mother, who was sitting in a rocking chair on the front porch of their now Hawkstown home. Oda removed her glasses and wiped her eyes. The two women wept silently together, for it had been a year since Russ had been killed in Belgium. This was one sad moment among many, many sad moments Oda experienced over the months and now years since Russ left home. There was relief at knowing where Russ was buried, because it meant they could pursue bringing him home with more information. However, the task was not over yet…and neither were the sad moments.

The letters continued.

January 31, 1946
Dear Sir,
Thank you for the information about where my son, Russell, is buried.
We are looking to get some pictures of the cemetery there in Belgium. Do
you think that I could get at least one so I would know where my son lays?
Sincerely,
Oda O. Gilley

April, 12 1946
Dear Mrs. Gilley,
Please find enclosed two pictures of the Henri Chapelle Cemetery as per
your request. I have no further information about the final disposition of
the remains of your son who died in battle defending our country.
My warmest personal regards to you and your family.
Major Henry Frank

August 15, 1946
Dear Sir,
I continue to wonder about my boy, Russell J. Gilley, who died at the
Battle of the Bulge and is buried at Herni Chapelle Cemetery in Belgium.
Do you have any information regarding my wish to bring him home?
Sincerely,
Oda O. Gilley

November 14, 1946
Dear Mrs. Gilley,
We have received your letter and in fact I have all the letters you have
written here in your son's file. You can be assured that the appropriate per-
sonnel are very much aware of your son's file and your continuing concern.
You may also be assured that the United States Government is fully com-

mitted to bringing home all the men who fell in battle and are buried over-seas if their families so desire.

We will be back in touch in due time.

Sincerely,

Major Henry Frank

January 10, 1947
Dear Sir,
I received you letter in November but have heard nothing yet about the plans to bring my son, Russell J. Gilley, home. Is there anything I should be doing to help you?
Sincerely,
Oda O. Gilley

March 11, 1947
Dear Mrs. Gilley,
Your letter concerning your son, the late Private First Class Russell J. Gilley, has been received in this office. The War department has now been authorized to remove the remains of our honored, at Government expense, to the final resting place, which the next of kin may designate.

When the necessary verification of record has been completed a "Letter of Inquiry—Return of World War II Dead" will be mailed to you. Until you receive this letter of inquiry it will not be necessary for you to contact this office again. Every effort will be made to shorten the time between now and the date of mailing and your desires will be acted on with a minimum of delay.

As you requested, enclosed are copies of "Tell Me about My Boy" and "Summary of Information on Final Burial of World War II Dead."
Sincerely,
James L. Prenn, Major
QMC, Memorial Division.

August 17, 1947
Dear Sir, I am very sorry to bother you again but I want you to know that my first son, Woodrow C. Gilley, will handle all arrangements for the reburial (here in Virginia) of my baby son Russell J. Gilley who died at the Battle of the Bulge in January 1945. He is fully authorized to act on my behalf.
Sincerely,

Oda O. Gilley

October 28, 1947
Dear Sir,
I am very sorry to bother you for I know you are very busy…but I have been very dissatisfied with the form "Request for Disposition of Remains" for my son Russell Gilley, who died in Belgium on January 16, 1945. I want my son back for burial in the U. S. and am frustrated that so many of my letters are getting me nowhere. If you have any idea about when he will be brought back to the United States for burial I would appreciate knowing.
Sincerely yours, Oda O. Gilley.

November 21, 1947
Dear Mrs. Gilley,
We are very sorry for all of your grief and want to ensure that your wishes are recognized fully by the Army.
The attached Disinterment Directive provides additional information for you.
Sincerely,
Col Franklin Smith

DISINTERMENT DIRECTIVE: 05-08-47

Consignee: WOODROW C. GILLEY, FRIES, VIRGINIA
Nature of Burial;   MATTRESS COVER
Conditions of remains: EXTREMITIES DISARTICULATED, BODY IN FINAL STAGE OF DECOMPOSITION.
Means of identification: NONE
Minor Discrepancies: ID AND "GRS TAG" HAVE NO MIDDLE INITIAL 'J'.
Remains Placed in Casket: 2 October 1947

RECEIPT OF REMAINS, December 15, 1947.
Remains Consigned to: *WOODROW C. GILLEY, FRIES, VIR-*
GINIA

REMAINS OF LATE PRIVATE FIRST CLASS RUSSELL J. GIL-
LEY SN 32 218 032 WILL BE DELIVERD TO YOU EIGHTEEN
DECEMBER BY GOVERNMENT MOTORCAR ACCOMPANIED
BY ESCORT CORPORAL JOHN S. BORD. REMAINS WILL
DEPART FROM THIS DISTRIBUTION CENTER AT TEN AM
AND WILL ARRIVE ON OR ABOUT FOUR PM. REQUEST YOU
MAKE ARRANGEMENT TO ACCEPT REMAINS UPON DELIV-
ERY.
FREDERIC W. DENIS, JR., LT COL, QMC

SIGNED AS ACCEPTING: Woodrow C. Gilley, 17 December 1947

On the evening of December 16, 1947, Oda sat in her living room
in the new Hawkstown house Wood had built for her using a part of
the $10,000 benefit she and Reba received following Russ's death. She,
Reba and Wood were discussing her plans for Russ's body. It was now
almost three years to the day since Hitler had begun the Battle of the
Bulge. The years since had been a long and tortuous journey for Oda
and all of her family to bring Russ home.

"You know I'll probably have to have him reburied once again when
we get the plots straight at Saddle Creek Church," Oda responded to
Wood in her way of announcing her intentions.

"Yes," he agreed, "you need to bring Daddy over from North Carolina, so you'll need more space for you and him—and Russ."

"So we'll bury him there by himself for now," she assented, looking
at her children. "You all better understand that that is his place."

"Yes, Mom," Wood and Reba agreed, though Wood squirmed a little. He could see by the look in Oda's eye that there was something
more to this. Possibly something he wouldn't like.

Sure enough, after a moment she asked, "Wood."

"Yes, Mom."

"When he gets here we'll need to make sure."

Startled, thirty-six-year-old Wood asked, "Sure of what?" There was anxiety in his usually calm voice.

"Well, you remember the reports there weren't any positive identification. No dog tags. How do we know?"

Wood winced, seeing where she was going. "Will we ever know for sure?"

"We need to find out."

"How?"

"I need you to open the casket and look and see what you think."

The tension in the air heightened dramatically, for both Oda and her mountain of a son knew that the body was reported to be absent extremities—arms and legs—and badly decomposed.

Wood didn't want to look. What difference did it make? They were all convinced beyond a shadow of a doubt that Russ was dead, and that this was most likely his body. Not Oda, she was not as certain. He cleared his throat and rubbed at his eyes. "Mom. Mom, I don't know if I can do it."

"Yes, you can. You're the strong one. You went and got your daddy's body when he died, and you were younger then. You can do this," she instructed him calmly, with a determination that none of her children could deny.

Tears trickled down Wood's cheeks. "Can Bill come with me?"

"No," she replied. "No use to involve anybody else. This is for you and me. And we can do it."

That night, as my daddy Wood and I rode home in his '41 Mercury Coupe, he seemed disoriented and at times I, his nine year-old son, thought he was going to have what my mountain momma would have called a fit (or, as it might later to be known, a "panic attack"). He was in a state of major distress, now that I look back on it. Some of his and Oda's kin suffered from depression, bipolar disorder and panic attacks, but I had never thought about it as far as my daddy was concerned. He was a mountain of strength—a virtual pillar for the entire Gilley family. He was very nervous that night, because of what his mother had asked him to do.

By the time Russ's body arrived on December 17, 1947, his eldest brother had regained his composure and was steeled to look in that casket. I am certain that he wished that Doug, Bill or Foy could be with him at least for moral support but at the temporary funeral home in the freight room of the Fries Train Station he was told that he had to go in alone and Oda wanted only him to do it no use for others to see her baby's condition

Then daddy left the car alone and went into the station. The workers present hauled the casket into the freight room from the special Hearse that brought it from Charlotte. Then the door closed behind them and stayed that way for the longest time. Or so it seemed to a nine year old.

Finally, daddy emerged, red faced and anxious, and jumped into the car. He sat there for a few minutes gathering his composure before he looked over at his companion. "It's Russ," he assured himself—and me or so it seemed. "It's Russ."

That was the end of that, or so he thought.

After the casket was transferred back to the hearse Woodrow Gilley led the way for the procession in our car. I sat in the back seat with the Corporal, who had accompanied Russ' body from Charlotte. The hearse followed, and behind it stretched a line of more than a hundred cars, as Momma later told me. Oda and Reba rode with Rube and Foy who drove and followed the hearse.

Foy, a former U. S. Army MP who had helped clean up a concentration camp in Europe at the end of the war, drove in his stoic way looking straight ahead never uttering an unnecessary word. He never spoke seriously about his experiences in Germany and Poland; it had been a shock to his system from which many thought he never recovered. The car behind them carried Pearl and her husband, Doug, who had been shell shocked when a mortar landed in the foxhole he was sharing with other GIs—who didn't make it. Doug lived a full life in terms of years and family, but he, too, never really recovered from the war.

The procession traveled down Main Street in Fries; past the high school Russ had quit in the 9th grade. All the cars had their lights on as the dusk descended on that Blue Ridge mountain community in mid December. Daddy turned left and went up the rock and gravel (and mud) Hilltown Road, for he had chosen to take Russ past our house on the way to Hawkstown rather than the more direct way up old route 94. It was symbolic.

The long caravan of cars with lights on reached the crest of the rise where the Hill family, my mother's people, had built their homes two generations earlier. With the coming of well drilling they had shifted from being hollow dwellers dependent on fresh water springs, and had built a row of one, two and three bedroom clapboard houses with out-houses and pumps. There, Momma and I had more than two hundred aunts, uncles, cousins and other relatives.

Word had spread that Russ was coming home, finally, and he was coming through this community. Each porch held a small group of people—mothers, fathers and children. Many parents held their smaller children up high on their hips for a better view, so the young ones would remember that day and remember the true cost of war. Years later, several of my cousins who had been no more than five on that day recalled the procession of automobiles and headlights moving slowly through the community.

Several of the people held candles, and as the hearse went by, they slowly raised the flickering flames as if to say, *Russ you're home now and we know you're in heaven. We salute you and grieve with your mother but we know you are at peace.*

They reached the end of Hilltown Road; turned left onto the hard surfaced Route 94 and continued on for a half mile to Oda's and Reba's new home in Hawkstown. There, I was surprised to see dozens of other cars parked with their headlights on, waiting to join the procession.

The roads were blocked each way as the hearse stopped and pulled into the driveway.

Russ's relatives and friends who had been asked to serve as official pallbearers helped get the casket out of the hearse and into the living room, where it stayed for the night. Oda didn't open it, of course, instead she accepted Wood's assertion that was her son Russ, a fact that both relieved her and wiped all hope away. Oda sank into despair once again that evening.

Wood, Forest and their nine-year-old son went home to be with Mickey (who had stayed most of the day with first cousin, Betty Jane Hill.) Other friends and family members stayed sitting with Russ's casket throughout the night. The next morning, many cars made the forty-five minute drive up Route 94 to where it met the old New River at the Riverside Café. There, the caravan turned right and wound its way up the river through Grayson County to the Saddle Creek Primitive Baptist Church, where Russ's funeral was held in an over flowing sanctuary with a minister of Oda's choosing giving the eulogy and he was laid to rest in the grave Oda had picked for him. The only representative of the Army was the Corporal but many veterans came to pay their last respects to a mountain boy who had fought for his country.

◆   ◆   ◆

Still, Oda wasn't satisfied. Her baby boy, her favorite son, was gone. The Germans had killed Russ and she would never forgive them. She cheered when Truman ended the war in the Pacific but that still wasn't enough for her.

"Why, Mom?" Reba quietly asked one evening as they sat at home on their front porch.

"Why? What?"

"Why keep on with this? It's hurting you, you're so down, and it ain't helping anybody, much less Russ. He loved you. You loved him. He died with the bible you gave him, so we know; we know that he was right with the Lord." After a long silence, Reba continued, "We all have to go sometime. This is just the first step in eternity. You know that. Russ is waiting for us. Please, Mom, let it go. I'm worried about you."

"I know," the old woman replied. "I know it was my fault and I ain't going to ever get over it."

"It wasn't your fault," Reba insisted with a gentle emphasis. "We've been over that a dozen times. Russ always had his way with you. You whipped him and locked him in his room, but he was so strong headed, so determined to go. He wanted to go."

"I know but he went and I had him pulled out and then let him go back. I made the biggest mistake of my life."

"Yes, Momma," Reba continued. "We all wish we had done something different. Wood does. I do. I promised you long ago that I'd look out after Russ. I should have." Tears welled up in her eyes.

Oda looked at her daughter with eyes that were already red from rubbing, and assured Reba, "No, it was my fault, and every time I look at the Gold Star I realize why I have it and why I keep it."

"We can't do anything now," Reba concluded.

"I am doing something."

"What?"

"I bought another grave plot. I aim to move Russ."

"Mom, move him?"

"Yes, move him."

"Why?"

"Well I've been talking to Russ a lot lately you know and we've come to an agreement."

"An agreement?"

"Yes, we need to stay close. Webb is at peace but Russ and me; we need to keep each other company. I want to be there for him."

◆   ◆   ◆

In July 1971, Oda Osborne Gilley lay dying at the farm she and Reba had bought when they sold the Hawkstown house in the early 1950s. Many members of the family gathered that weekend, including me, the grandson who had been with her when the word came that Russell was dead, that fateful January day in 1945. Now, her grandson Wade was with her again, as was his son, seven-month-old Wade Jr.

Reba was unknowingly suffering from diabetes and would shortly follow her mother due to kidney failure. But that was yet in the future. On seeing Wade Jr., Reba smiled wide and took him in her arms with obvious joy. The baby boy was Oda's only great grandson to carry the Gilley name. Knowing how this mattered to her momma, she carried the baby into the bedroom, where Oda lay on her deathbed. The old woman had not spoken for weeks as she slowly but surely faded, for after all she was past the biblical fourscore cited as a lifespan by the Primitive Baptists. She was sinking into a permanent state where she would join Webb and Russ in that next world, which had become so important to her in the past few years.

Reba thought seeing her great grandson might rouse Oda to speak, might bring her out of the shadowy coma that held sway. Reba leaned over and held the baby directly in front of Oda's face. "Mom, look at what I got. Look here Mom. It's Wade's baby boy. It's Wade Jr."

The eyelids of the aged, tired woman fluttered. For the first time in days, she opened her eyes and stared at the baby. There was a deep darkness about those Cherokee eyes as they widened and focused alertly.

Reba had been right about the baby. Oda stared at Wade Jr. for several minutes while the others in the room stood transfixed by the scene. Her mouth moved as though she would speak, though she hadn't spoken for weeks.

Finally, she moistened her lips and whispered, "He's white headed, just like my boys. Just like Russ."

Then for the first time in months, Oda's eyes were open and she seemed to smile for herself. She smiled as she once again drifted off in to that other existence. She had seen the next generation and it was pleasing.

◆   ◆   ◆

Oda Gilley passed on later that week. Rather, according to her faith, she traveled to another world where she would wait for her family to gather around her once again.

According to her wishes, Oda was buried in the Saddle Creek Primitive Baptist Church in upper Grayson County, Virginia. On a hillside near the birth waters of the world's oldest river, the New River, Oda was laid to rest beside her Russ, who had died twenty-six years earlier in Belgium. She had arranged to have herself buried with her son instead of her husband, Webb, who was still in his grave in North Carolina.

Oda had earned her Gold Star, and then she'd taken it a step further, joining her son at his side.

Authors Note One

Ilas Gallimore, of Galax, Virginia, a boyhood friend of Russell Gilley wrote a letter to me in the fall of 2003. This is some of what he wrote in that letter, in his own words.

Big Boy Gilley...My Friend

Russell James Gilley and I grew up together in Eagle Bottom, Virginia. We walked to school together and went to the movies in Fries together. When we would play football Russ would carry the ball and I would tackle one leg. Then two or three guys would jump on his back and we would finally get him down...

Russ liked being with friends. Sometimes going home from school, we would walk up thru Hilltown so we could walk and talk to our friends. Russ's big brother Woodrow had married one of those Hill girls and lived up there. Russ liked to see him.

Finally one day it came to me. When we were young Bill and Russ and I were out playing and Russ and I were trying to box. I got lucky and gave Russ a bloody nose. Russ said with a sullen look, "I always said any man that ever brought blood from me I would kill him." I came back at him, "Come on Big Boy I think I can handle you." Russ looked at me and smiled and then laughed out loud and walked away.

Bill didn't know the whole story. I knew that Russ wouldn't want to hurt me because if he did my mother might stop giving him dimes so he could go to the movies with me. Bill Criner had thought all these years that I had backed Big Boy Gilley down.

Russ, Bill Criner and I were at the Church of God in Eagle Bottom. We were out in the parking lot where there was an old model car, open top, a 1928 or 29 Star. Russ said, run over to that woodpile and bring us a block of that wood. So I did. Russ and Bill lifted up the hind wheels. I placed the block of wood under the axle housing and then we went across the road and hid behind a fodder shock. When church

121

broke up they came out and loaded up in the car. Then the driver said, "My car won't move." Then they all unloaded. Some were saying put it in second; others said try it in reverse. It was very dark. Then someone said this wheel is turning. Someone else said there is something scraping my foot. Finally they figured out what had happened and got enough men and women to lift it up and off the block. I was afraid they might get mad but the night was quiet. We could hear them driving off up the road laughing.

Russ and I were coming up old Route 11 in an old model 1937 Dodge. I bought it from Square Taylor. It had been sitting in place for about two years and the tires looked like they were rotten. Russ saw a bunch of sailors standing by the road and wanted to give them a ride. I said, "We can't my tires are rotten and we can't haul them all." But Russ said, "If they can't all get in here and ride, I will get out and walk." So, I pulled over. Four got in the back seat. Russ was yelling like he was loading cattle. He had one sailor crawl in and lay across the laps of the ones seated and placed another on the floor at their feet. One sat between Russ and me in the front seat. However there was one left standing. He was small, looked like he might weigh about seventy-five pounds. Russ yelled, "Come here you little guy you can sit on my lap". It was good that the highway was straight because I had no room to turn the steering wheel. We had to help them unload. They had laughed all the way as we drove and were laughing when we left them as they waved goodbye. Russ called out to them; "I'll be with you boys in a couple more months." Russ said, "You see I told you that if I couldn't get them all in here I would get out and walk."

Money for a moving picture show ticket was hard to come by. Sometimes Russ would borrow a dime from my Mother. He liked to see Gene Autry in movies. Most movies would include a newsreel called Time Marches On. It seemed like we would soon be in a war. We talked about this as we walked home to Eagle Bottom after the show in Fries. Russ would say that we are soon going to be in a war and you and I are going to be just frying size.

He showed me something one night as we were walking home about the moon that old people claimed was a sign of war. He said, "I'll be glad to go because I want to die for my country. Dying for your country is the greatest honor that can be bestowed upon a man. I want to be a machine gunner. Do you know the average life of a machine gunner?" I told him that I had no idea. He said, "Nineteen minutes and when you hear that I have been killed you can be sure that I took ten or fifteen with me."

One time he said, "I wish you and I could go together". I said, "I don't want to go with you because you want to get killed for your country and take me with you. I'll go when they call me but I hope to come back." I told him about all the good things we could do after the war was over and that one hundred years from now people will forget that there was ever a Russ Gilley. I lived with the hope that he might change his mind when he got there in the war.

One time Russ was in on leave and he came down to my house. I told him I was sorry, "I have no money and no car. If I did we would do some running around." He said, "That's alright let's just walk around." It was getting dark and we walked very slow up to Stevens Creek and on up to Liberty Hill. We talked about girls we knew and about the war.

He said, "I am in the 99th the fightinest bunch of SOBs that ever lived." That's when he showed me on his shoulder nine little blocks one way and nine the other way—the 99th. It was very late when we got back to Eagle Bottom that night. He gave me a picture of him and his friend.

I once talked to the late Clinerd Anders after I moved back in 1989. He was with Russ in the War. He said Russell didn't try to take care of himself. He wanted to fight so much.

After I got out of the military, I got married and went to Maryland in 1949. I came back to Fries in 1989 and soon ran into Bill Criner. He told me about Russ and his war experience. I thought to myself, that was what Russ told me he was going to do before the war even started.

I passed his grave this past summer going to Shatley Springs. I am sorry he gave his life for his country but I feel honored that I grew up with him.

Author's Note Two

In 1999, I received a letter from the Mayor of Fries, Virginia—Carolyn Jones. Mrs. Jones wrote and forwarded a letter about my uncle Russ Gilley that she had received several weeks earlier. She wrote that I was the only surviving relative of Russ Gilley that she knew how to contact. The letter was from a man in Belgium by the name of J. L. Seel and it concerned Russ.

It seems that Mr. Seel, whose email address is or was <u>digger@ skynet.be</u>, is something of an unofficial guardian of the Elsenborn Ridge Battle field in Belgium where the U. S. Army 99th Infantry Division had so valiantly fought the Germans during the Battle of the Bulge. Mr. Seel and an associate while investigating a section of the ridge where the battle was the fieriest, with the assistance of a metal detector, found several dog tags belonging to American soldiers.

Further investigation revealed that one of the dog tags belonged to my uncle Russ. Seel was writing to secure confirmation of the burial place of Russ Gilley as well as photographs of him and his tombstone to be placed in a museum at the battlefield as a memorial to American soldiers who died repelling the fierce and daring German adventure that could have turned the war or at least prolonged it for years and cause millions more deaths.

This was the first inkling of my knowing that Russ's dog tags were not previously found making the identity of the body received that cold December in 1947 less than certain. Apparently though Oda knew this fact and needed additional self-assurance that the body she would be burying was in fact that of her baby son. She assured herself by instructing her oldest son, Woodrow, to actually look at the remains, which had been buried in Belgium in a shallow grave for nearly three years and wrapped in the mattress on which he died.

Authors Note Three

ODA: My Grandmother

At times, a special relationship exists between a child and a grandparent, a relationship that is more than parental love. In those special cases, because of their shared life experiences, a unique bonding occurs.

Such was my own relationship with my father's mother, Oda Osborne Gilley. Oda was a woman of strong will, with strong opinions some say shaped by her Western North Carolina mountain early home life; and perhaps, her Cherokee heritage. Our relationship developed during the unsettled years of World War II and lasted through the rest of her life and, in a special way, my life. Our relationship was founded on the hard lessons she had learned in life and her love for her own. My relationship with Oda was far different from that I shared with my wonderful mother and that special relationship helped to guide me through an early childhood in Virginia's Blue Ridge Mountains and far beyond.

Oda Gilley suffered much in her lifetime. She lost her mother shortly after she was born, was raised by an uncle and then married an itinerant lumberman and tenant farmer much younger than herself. She immediately had seven children in thirteen years and had to move them frequently from job to job and place to place. Oda lost her husband in 1934 in the depths of the Great Depression leaving her with seven children still in school.

Oda also suffered from Pellagra, a nutritional deficiency that was common in the south in the years before the war. For much of her adult life, even beyond when she had to, Oda kept to her rigid Pellagra diet which eventually landed her at a hospital with collapsed bowels after more than twenty years. Through all this, she remained as strong as an oak tree, undaunted by it all.

Oda's life and lifestyle gave her deep concern for the future here on earth and a sincere confidence in the hereafter. Her mindset was mysterious to me as a child and is a matter of wonderment until this day. I remember going to Primitive Baptist (my mother called them Hard Shell Baptists) services and revivals and following her lead at all times. The churches she attended had Sunday services once a month, rather than every Sunday like many churches, but that service was an all day affair, including dinner on the ground. They did everything any church would do over the course of a week or month but all on that one Sunday. Granny Oda took me to a few of those and I was more comfortable in the blend of religion and social activities than my mother's Southern Baptist church.

However, I am convinced that her inner strength came from more than surviving hard times or being an old fashioned Baptist. It came from a deeper and more fundamental perception of the world and life, and when she turned to those depths in our conversations I, as a young boy, was…well, uneasy…And I still vividly remember those experiences and feelings. That is another whole other story.

The following story, to a degree, illustrates who Oda was and how our relationship developed.

Lye Soap and Soap Operas

I walked to the door leading to the open-air basement, or under-house, of Granny Oda Eagle Bottom home, and looked around for a long, long minute making sure I was not being watched. Then I slammed the door shut, locking Oda and her daughters Pearl and Reba inside.

The three women stopped talking and turned to look at the closed door. Reba shouted, "Wade, what do you think you are doing? What are you doing???"

I peered through the lattice that formed the walls of the ground level basement and storage room at the women and giggled out loud. I had caught them distracted and now they would play with me whether they wanted to or not.

Reba reacted immediately before Oda and Pearl comprehended what had happened, "Wade, you come here and unlock this door. Now! Right this minute!" She knew that they needed out of the basement and then!

Peering through the lattice, I was excited because they were excited and because I had become bored with all the scurrying around getting ready to make the lye soap. Full of my five years and having a close relationship with the three I laughed and replied, "Don't have the key! Don't have the key!" They knew that I was laughing without making a peep from the look on my face and that served to alarm them even more.

It was true; I didn't have the key to the lock, which was hanging loose on the door just out of my reach....And theirs. That day Oda and three of her daughters were busy making lye soap in a big black iron kettle hanging from the top of a tripod of iron rods over a hot wood fire in the level part of the yard on the north side of Granny's house. The three women had gone inside the open-air basement to look for some glass jars and other containers. They were so engrossed in discussing the potential of this jar and that jar that they had not noticed me or thought anything about the possibilities of being locked in that basement. Granny's other daughter, Ruby, (or Rube as we called her) had been sent up to her house next door for some glass jars and was not present at the time that I had locked the door.

Granny was keeping me, a five-year-old towhead, while my Momma worked the day shift in the Fries cotton mill. Ruby's husband, Foy, and Pearl's husband, Doug, were both away in the U.S. Army at this time. Russ, Granny's youngest son, had just finished basic training and left for Europe a few days earlier as the Allies prepared for a major offensive against the Nazis. So the women had decided to make soap that was something that needed to be done and something to keep their minds off what might be happening far away in Europe.

Making lye soap was a cost effective exercise and like many activities in those times it was also a social thing. It was a time to work and wait and while waiting to talk and tell stories. In fact, lye soap making, an art in colonial times, had been revived during the Great Depression. It cost much less for families with more time than money to make their own soap than to buy it from Proctor and Gamble. (Mr. Proctor and Mr. Gamble had, almost a hundred years earlier, through their ingenuity and the marvels of the industrial revolution, made soap that was so inexpensive that most Americans bought rather than made their own soap after the 1850s, but during this World War in the hill country of Virginia, it was well worth the effort.)

The making of lye soap was not easy. First the women had to get the ingredients, including lots of animal fat and the lye itself. Lye could be bought in most stores in tin cans, or it could be made at home by pouring water through wood ashes, which resulted in a very acidic solution or lye. The lye was mixed with scraps of animal fat and skin left over from killing hogs or cattle (for food) and placed in a large metal kettle over a fire outside. This mixture was cooked for some time until it formed soap. While the soap was being made, the women had sufficient idle time between the steps to gossip. Some people believe that soap making and the stories are associated with the name given to the new serialized radio programs of the 1930s known as "Soap Operas" or just "Soaps." I once read that, by 1940, more than forty percent of all adult women listed to these radio dramas or Soap Operas on a daily basis.

A "soap opera" was going on in real time in Granny's open-air basement that day and for a moment it was much to my delight. For while Oda and her daughters were locked in the open-air basement, the lye soap they were cooking cooked, cooked and, then, over cooked. Before long there was a certain and distinctive smell coming from the boiling pot as the soap burned and then overflowed into the fire. Then the seriousness of the situation and my precarious position began to dawn on me.

This was trouble, big time trouble…for me. And I knew about getting in trouble.

Soon, Rube showed up and saw what was happening. She bellowed at me, "Wade, what did you do? Where's the key? You come here right nooow…and help me!"

Granny got Rube's attention and told her where to find the key. Shehe came bounding down the steps into the yard, grabbed the master lock key from the nail and ran to unlock the basement door. Out of the under house burst Granny, Reba and Pearl all having unkind words and harsh looks for me. The three younger women hurried to the smoking, smelling soap while Granny turned her attention to me and I could tell what she was thinking. She stopped for a second to grab a small tree branch lying on the ground near the kettle and started moving in my direction with obvious determination. She was fast for an old woman in an ankle length blue skirt and red sweater. And she was mad. I turned and scampered away from my old grandmother (53 sure looked old then) by running up the hillside toward Rube's house.

Rube's house was another six-room dwelling with two bedrooms upstairs, perched on a little hill just north of Granny's house. In between was a small branch, which became larger for a while after each major rainfall and a ditch better known as a gully. I ran and ran and ran down into the gully and up the other side. Then just as I started up the hill, my angry Granny caught me and I got one real whipping with that tree branch, a whipping I wouldremember sixty years later.

As Granny administered justice (her definition) she told me again and again why she was doing it. She kept telling me, "This hurts me more than you." Then she marched me down the hillside back to her house as I cried and rubbed my eyes. For the rest of the afternoon, I sat on the front porch in semi-isolation watching while the women cleaned up the mess and saved as much lye soap as possible. There was no going inside and no going down the stairs to the yard. I felt like a pariah. There was no going anywhere that afternoon as per Granny's orders.

Much later, after a day of being deliberately ignored by my aunts and grandmother, my mother picked me up. Granny met her car at the road and they had an extensive and intensive discussion with much hand waving by both women. I had messed up, and now I was going to hear about it again and again. Momma was not one to let a guy forget a mistake. All the way home, an automobile ride of some twenty minutes, she was calm. She asked me lots of questions, but none that let to a discussion of the afternoon events. She would get to that in due time.

Momma had nothing, nothing at all—on the way home or ever.

On arriving home that day we carried on as if nothing had ever happened. She never brought the incident up. You see she respected Granny, but she was independent and not one of Oda's daughters and didn't normally defer to her. She was Forest Gladys Hill Gilley, first and foremost a Hill from Hilltown, and then, and only then, a Gilley. In that part of the World a Hill didn't defer to anyone, including a mother-in-law

Then, before I knew it, it was morning again. We were up bright and early at six o'clock eating breakfast before jumping into Momma's 1937 Chevrolet to drive over to Granny's house for another long day while Momma worked in the mill. For obvious reasons, I was not excited about spending that day at Granny's house. When I arrived Granny was polite, if somewhat cool, and so it went for most of the morning. We just sat in the sitting room as she did some mending, looked at what was cooking on the wood stove and let me attempt to read those books Momma always seemed to have around for me in my idle time.

The day dragged on and on, and I became more and more bored. There was an uneasiness or tension in the air, or so it seemed to me. The time I spent sitting in that small room with Granny was in many ways more painful than the whipping I had experienced the previous afternoon. The day seemed to move ever so slowly. The morning was endless.

Then, just before mid-day just at the time we would normally eat lunch, my Granny came in the living room, where I was sitting reading a book, looked at me in her unique, intense and unforgiving way and asked, "Wade, would you like to have a picnic?"

This was unusual, for Granny never seemed to do anything just for fun or leisure. I soon concluded that having a picnic would sure be better than what we were doing, just sitting around the house with a tension in the air thick enough to be cut with a butter knife. So I agreed, with great and real enthusiasm, "Sure. Let's go." Then I asked, "Where are we going to have a picnic, Granny?"

"We'll go to the top of the hill," she said, pointing to the hill rising behind her house. At that point in my life, all five years of it, that hill seemed to be a mountain.

And so we picnicked. First, she packed a worn, woven wicker basket with food and other things needed for a picnic, and then we climbed the little hill that overlooked all of Eagle Bottom. It was one of the few times I ever climbed that hill and saw all of the Bottom in one perspective, even though I made many trips to that community over the years continuing through my high school days. It was a beautiful day in those Blue Ridge Mountains of Virginia and it seemed that we could see forever looking out over the hills and hollers and streams.

Granny stopped in a field at the hilltop, spread out a blanket and sat down. Then she patted a spot on the blanket by her side with a dark and strong hand and said, "Come over here, Wade, and we'll eat."

I sat down with her, watching as she opened the basket and pulled out sliced tomatoes in wax paper and saltine crackers in their bag along with a quart jar of well water. We each ate several of the sandwiches—saltines with thick slices of red ripe tomato—while she explained what I had done that was so wrong the day before and why she had given me the whipping. To hear it told from her perspective everything made perfect sense. However, I admit that, at that time, I was dubious about the need for the switching. (Later when I had kids of my own it was different.)

I had gotten in trouble without knowing why and she had to make a point of it to teach me a life's lesson. It seemed that one of Granny's missions in life was to teach hard lessons about life and she was good at that.

As we began to get ready to leave the hilltop, I edged closer and told her, "Granny, I am sorry for doing that. And I ran away because I was scared." This was not the first but rather just one of many confessions I would give during the course of my life.

She didn't smile but now looking back, I realize there seemed to be a hint of acknowledgement and humor in her voice and, maybe, just maybe, a sparkle in her eyes as she accepted my apology. I had done wrong and admitted it.

I was truly sorry, and she took my hand as we walked back down the hill together. We must have made quite a pair. She was a slim dark woman of Cherokee decent, dressed in a long skirt hanging down to her shoe tops, with waist length black hair tied up in a bun on the back of her head. Her stride even had a certain authority about it and her hand provided a strong, reassuring grip. Holding to Oda Osborne Gilley's hand I was a five-year-old, with light brown (piss burnt brown I later learned) hair, son of her first son and grandson of her husband who had died some ten years earlier. It was easy walking down that hill that day; in fact it was like walking on a cloud.

Russ in the Army

Oda Gilley, 1907

Russ and Reba at School——First Grade

Russ and Reba School Picture

Russ, Rex and Reba in Eaglebottom

Reba and Russ as Teenagers

Russ and Sister Pearl

Russ in High School

Reba and Ruby

Russ and Two Fellow Gis

Elsenborn Ridge in Early 1945

Hattie, Bill, Wood and Forest Gilley

Church Where Russ and Oda are Buried

Oda at Russ's Grave at Saddle Creek

Oda and Belle

Webb Gilley in 1931

Wade Gilley in 1945

Oda Gilley and Rex in 1962

Oda and Five Grandsons 1962

Oda's Grandchildren and Some spouses

Fries Cotton Mill Dam at Flood Stage

Hilltown

Eaglebottom and Area Outside Fries

Wade's Family

New River Valley

The Author

Wade Gilley is the nephew of Russell "Russ" Gilley and the grandson of Oda Osborne Gilley, the principal characters in this story from World War II. Wade Gilley, born in 1938, was staying with his grandmother during the latter days of the war. Here he shares intimate and vivid memories of her before and after his uncle's death, a tragedy that was to haunt her for the remainder of her life. The connection between Wade and his grandmother was powerful and lifelong. It was she who encouraged him to attend college and eventually become an engineer and author.

In *Damn Right It Hurts*, although Wade does not flinch from portraying his grandmother as the uncompromising, switch-wielding, dominating matriarch she was, he remembers her also as a woman who struggled against overwhelming odds all of her life and who loved her family with every ounce of her being.

0-595-32094-5

Printed in the United States
22877LVS00004B/178-255

9 780595 320943